I stood up so quickly I knocked my desk chair over. A horrible feeling pierced through me.

Where was the doll?

"Jesse? You all right?" my dad asked.

"I—" I began.

But I didn't get a chance to finish. Suddenly, we heard a scream and a thumping noise.

Dad and I rushed out into the hall and toward the stairs. Mom was lying all twisted at the bottom.

"Eve!" Dad yelled. He started down the stairs toward her. I was right behind him.

But I stopped at the landing halfway down. The Mrs. Fink doll sat leaning against the banister. Her blank gaze was pure evil.

The doll had pushed Mom down the stairs!

**Read these books in
the SHADOW ZONE series:**

**And zapping your way from
the SHADOW ZONE soon:**

SHADOW ZONE™

MY TEACHER ATE MY HOMEWORK

BY J. R. BLACK

BULLSEYE BOOKS

Random House New York

1

Teacher Creature

On an ordinary Tuesday morning it hit me. I finally figured out why my life was totally messed up.

I had landed in some kind of time warp!

It hung over my hometown of Cape Sorrow, North Carolina, like a storm front that wouldn't budge. No matter what I did, I stayed stuck.

Because tell me this: If I always set my clock ten minutes fast, why was I always fifteen minutes behind?

"Jesse!" Dad stood in my doorway, frowning at me. "What are you doing still in bed? Annabel is wandering around in her pajamas."

"Sorry," I mumbled. "I guess the alarm didn't go off."

"Or maybe you turned it off and went back to sleep," Dad said. "Get a move on. I'll help Annabel. French toast for breakfast."

Dad shut the door with a sharp click. He's usually cranky in the mornings. First of all, he's never been what you'd call a morning person. Second, he was working nights.

Dad went on the graveyard shift at the furniture factory last fall when he and Mom opened a restaurant called the Blue Bay Cafe. They're both awesome cooks, and it had been their dream for years. The only trouble was, they couldn't afford to lose Dad's salary. So for the time being, Mom ran the restaurant while Dad continued to work at the furniture factory.

Now, Dad still could have worked during the day, but then there wouldn't have been anyone around to look after my six-year-old sister, Annabel, and me. By working two different shifts, one of them would always be home. Or at least that's what was supposed to happen.

Dad's hours were pretty regular. But Mom's job kept spilling over into her free time. In the mornings she woke up early to get down to the docks. She liked to buy fresh fish from the boats just coming in. And then in the afternoons she'd usually have to "run in and do a few things," which meant we didn't see her at all.

Not only did we not see much of Mom, we never saw Mom and Dad *together* anymore. Last

Christmas, Mom and Dad had decided to open the restaurant because they needed the business. Some Christmas. I ended up eating fried shrimp with Josie, the waitress. Annabel fell asleep with her new doll, and Mom and Dad waited tables.

Since Mom and Dad didn't see each other much, there was a lot of missed communication. Somebody always forgot to make lunch or do the laundry or pay a bill. Not to mention that my own chores had doubled. I had to watch out for Annabel fifty hours a day. And I was always late for something. Like school.

"Jesse?" Annabel peeked around my bedroom door as I pulled on a T-shirt.

"Didn't I tell you to knock?" I asked.

Annabel shut the door. I heard a soft knock.

"Who is it?" I said.

"It's Annabel," Annabel said.

"Who?" I teased.

"*Annabel!*" she yelled. I heard her foot stamp.

"Annabel who?" I said.

The door flew open. Annabel stood there with her hands on her hips. She looked just like Mom, except that she was about three feet tall. She had the same curly dark hair and big brown eyes. The same expression that said, *I'm losing patience with you, Jesse.*

"Dad says to come down to breakfast," Annabel said.

"C'mere," I said, noticing that one of her sneakers was untied. Annabel had dressed herself in her yellow overalls with a purple T-shirt. My little sister was the colorful type.

"You have to double knot it," I said, bending down and tying her sneaker. "Remember how I taught you?"

"I *know*," Annabel said, rolling her eyes. Ever since she'd started first grade, Annabel thought she was some kind of Einstein. Her eleven-year-old big brother couldn't teach her anything anymore.

We went downstairs to breakfast. Dad was starting to cheer up. He must have had his coffee. He was whistling while he made French toast.

"Mom's still asleep," Dad said. "Did you guys make your beds?"

"I'll do it after breakfast," I said.

"I thought I'd surprise Mom and go down with her to the docks today," Dad said. "I have to be downtown anyway to renew my driver's license. Then grocery shopping, and back home to make macaroni and cheese casserole for dinner. Which means I might not get to the laundry Think you can handle it while I'm sleeping, slugger? Just one load."

"I guess so," I said.

"You're a prince among men," Dad said, sliding a piece of French toast on my plate.

Annabel poked me. "You promised to fix my dollhouse," she said.

"I know," I answered. "I'll get to it."

"Would you pour Annabel some milk, Jesse?" Dad asked. He sliced a peach and fanned it out on Annabel's plate the way she liked it.

"Sure," I said. I reached for the milk.

Dad sat down with his coffee. "Put the casserole in a 350-degree oven at around five forty-five," he said to me. "I'll make the salad."

"Okay," I said.

He looked at his watch. "Eat up, kids. It's getting late. Jess, make sure Annabel really brushes, not just sucks on the bristles, okay?"

Mom dashed into the kitchen in her sweatshirt and jeans. She swiped a piece of peach off Annabel's plate. "The bluefish are running!" she said wildly. "I can't find my keys!"

And that's when the morning really got going. You see my problem?

I had fifty million things to do, and it wasn't even eight o'clock yet. And did I mention that I was running fifteen minutes behind?

"Sorry I'm late," I puffed to my best buddy, Cody Glimcher. I had run four blocks to meet him in front of his driveway.

"No problemo," he said. He got up and stuffed the book he was reading into his knapsack. He was probably getting a head start on an assignment. Cody was totally organized and got straight A's. I didn't hold it against him, though.

We started walking toward school. "So what's up since yesterday?" I said.

"Did you say something about birthdays?" Cody asked innocently.

I grinned. "Did I?" Tomorrow was Cody's birthday. He'd already reminded me about fifty times. He knew I always forgot things. But I'd already bought him his present, a new tool for his woodworking shop.

"My mom told me what I'm getting," Cody said. His orangey hair seemed to glow along with his big grin. "A mountain bike!"

"Totally cool," I said enviously. I'd wanted one for Christmas, but my parents said they couldn't afford it. Maybe for my birthday, they said. That wasn't till July. Now Cody would be zooming around for *months* while I puffed along on my pukey three-speed.

"I even get to pick it out," Cody said. "I'm totally psyched. You know that bike shop in St. Jude?"

I nodded. "They have stellar stuff."

St. Jude was the neighboring town. It was bigger than Cape Sorrow, and kind of touristy. Everyone went there for big purchases and Christmas shopping.

"Geneva said she'd drive me there this afternoon," Cody said. "Do you want to come and help me pick it out?"

"This afternoon?" I asked. I thought quickly. I had to do the laundry and pop the casserole in the oven. But on Tuesday afternoons, Annabel had swimming class, so I didn't have to babysit. I could definitely swing it. I could do my homework after Annabel went to bed. If I wasn't too tired.

"We'll be back by four-thirty," Cody said. "And if you're worried about Geneva's driving, she promised not to put on any of her weird tapes. She'll concentrate on the road."

Cody's teenage sister was a total space case. She was into crystals and t'ai chi and meditation. Last summer, she drove Cody and me to the state beach in St. Jude and *chanted* all the way there. I'm not kidding you.

"And she'll take us for pizza, too," Cody added.

"I'm there," I said. Then I poked Cody. "As long as I don't have detention again."

Cody's face clouded. "Did you bring your homework?" he asked worriedly. "El Finko will go ballistic if you didn't."

El Finko was what we called our awesomely awful teacher, Mrs. Augusta Fink. She'd been teaching sixth grade at our school for centuries. There was no telling how many kids she'd tortured. She had gray hair and mean little beady eyes and a mole on one cheek.

When we were studying "Our Neighbors to the South" in social studies last term, I'd pointed out to Cody how Mrs. Fink's mole was the exact shape of Brazil. We'd laughed hysterically for about ten minutes straight. I'd gotten detention for that one. Ever since then, we'd called Mrs. Fink El Finko. Behind her back, of course.

For some reason, Mrs. Fink had singled me out as the worst student in the class. Just because I daydreamed sometimes. And maybe misplaced my homework once or twice.

"No sweat, Cody," I said. "I have my English composition. And it's an A for sure."

8

Cody didn't look relieved. In fact, he looked kind of pale.

"So maybe it's a B," I said uneasily. "El Finko will freak when I hand it in on time."

"Jesse, our English composition isn't due until *Thursday*," Cody said.

"Oh," I said. "Well, then she'll *really* freak when I hand it in three days early. Maybe she'll have a heart attack." I clutched my chest and toppled over onto someone's lawn.

Cody looked down at me. "Our *history* paper is due today," he said. "On the Civil War."

"Oh," I said. I got up and dusted off my jeans. "Are you sure?" But who am I kidding? This was Mr. Organization talking.

Cody shook his head. "Boy, oh boy," he moaned. "When Mrs. Fink finds out you messed up again, you're going to be dead meat."

"Maybe she won't call on me today," I said.

Cody just shook his head. "Dead meat," he repeated.

2

Dead Meat

Iron gray eyes glinted behind steel-rimmed spectacles. The knifelike gaze slowly swept the classroom. I sank down in my chair.

"Who would like to go first?" Mrs. Fink asked.

I waited, hoping some A student would volunteer. But everybody was afraid of Mrs. Fink. Even Debbi Oleander, who did extra credit for *fun,* didn't raise her hand.

"It looks like I'll have to choose someone," Mrs. Fink said.

I ducked behind burly Burt Mackinac.

"How about..."

I made myself as small as possible. I considered dropping my pencil, but Mrs. Fink was on to that ploy. She'd call on me for sure.

"Cristina Spinola," Mrs. Fink said.

Whew. Cristina picked up her paper and nervously went to the head of the class. She started to read her paper on the Civil War battle of Antietam in a wobbly voice.

"That's An–*tee*-tam, not An–*tye*-tam, Cristina," Mrs. Fink suddenly barked. Cristina jumped. "What do I always say?"

"I don't know, Mrs. Fink," Cristina whispered, her dark eyes wide.

"If you're not sure how to pronounce something, look it up in the dictionary!" Mrs. Fink said. "Or ask me."

Cristina shrank against the blackboard. The expression on her face said she'd rather die than ask Mrs. Fink *anything*.

"Class, I've said this over and over again," Mrs. Fink said in a voice that dripped icicles. "The dictionary is your friend. Please use it. Now, Cristina, you may continue."

Cristina started to read again. The paper shook a little in her hand. I felt sorry for her. Cristina had just moved here from Portugal and was really shy.

But I couldn't help being glad it wasn't me.

Cristina finally finished. When she walked back to her seat, she had chalk all over the back of her navy jumper. She'd been pressing against the blackboard to get as far away as possible from Mrs. Fink. Who could blame her?

"Next," Mrs. Fink said. "How about..." Her eyes rested on me for a minute. I looked back steadily, as if I was saying, *You can pick me, Mrs. Fink. I'm totally prepared.*

"Peter Quigley?" Mrs. Fink called.

Saved again. For now.

But even I couldn't hold out forever. Even though I asked a trillion questions after Peter's boring report on the Gettysburg Address. Even though I finally resorted to the dropping-the-pencil routine. Even though I faked a sneezing fit. With only ten minutes to go until the bell, disaster struck.

"Jesse Hackett?"

I cleared my throat.

"Mr. Hackett? We're waiting."

"Actually, Mrs. Fink," I said, "I don't have my paper today. I got mixed up. I have my English composition, though." I waved it in the air hopefully.

Mrs. Fink drummed her long, knuckly fingers on her desk. "I see, Mr. Hackett. And I must say, as much as I might look forward to your stunning compositions, I can wait until the day they're due. Which in this case is Thursday."

The class tittered. What can I say? No loyalty.

Mrs. Fink's steely eyes drilled into me. "Are you aware that you are failing history, Mr.

Hackett? And that you are very much in danger of being left back?"

Thanks for telling the whole class, El Finko. Or should I say *gracias?* "Yes," I mumbled.

"So, knowing this, you came to class today empty-handed?" Mrs. Fink pursed her thin lips. "Are you also aware that your project will slip one full grade for being late?"

"Yes, Mrs. Fink," I said.

"My, my," Mrs. Fink said. She shook her head as though she couldn't believe what she was hearing. "You must have incredible confidence in the excellence of your paper, Mr. Hackett. We all look forward to hearing this masterpiece. I'm assuming, of course, that the paper is *done.*"

"It's done," I said. "I just forgot to bring it in."

"I see. Then it won't be any problem for you to copy out the Facts to Remember section of chapters eight and nine in your history book tonight. That might help with that memory problem."

"Yes, Mrs. Fink," I said. Cody shot me a despairing look.

I knew what he was thinking. How could I write a history paper, do a punishment assignment, *and* go with him to St. Jude?

Just watch me.

* * *

"Are you *sure,* Jesse?" Cody asked me at my locker after school.

"Sure I'm sure," I said, grabbing my denim jacket. "I'm not letting El Finko spoil my day. No way." I slammed my locker shut, wishing Mrs. Fink's gnarly hand was in the way.

"But you've got all that homework," Cody said. "I can pick out my bike myself."

"It's no sweat, Cody," I said. "Look, just because we snared the meanest person on planet Earth as our teacher doesn't mean we have to knuckle under. Can you believe she was so mean to Cristina today?"

"She just moved here from Portugal," Cody agreed. "How could she know how to pronounce 'Antietam'?"

"Mrs. Fink is pure evil," I said. "Haven't you heard the rumors? The older kids say that she was once the ringleader of a gang of pirates in the Bahamas. And someone else told me she started out working in an animal shelter. She's the one who gassed the puppies."

Cody snickered.

"But the real, true rumor is that her ex-husband was a mass murderer," I said. "But Mrs. Fink left *him* because he wasn't successful enough!"

I burst out laughing at my own joke. But I

didn't even get a giggle out of Cody. He looked like a deer frozen in somebody's headlights.

"Cody?" I whispered. "Is something wrong?"

Cody's eyes flickered to a spot past my shoulder.

I turned around.

Mrs. Fink was standing right behind me. She had heard every word I'd said!

3

Little Shop of Horror

Mrs. Fink and I locked eyes. Her face was completely white except for two red spots on her cheeks. She was really steamed.

Her mouth opened. Then it snapped shut with a *click*. She turned and stalked off.

"Whew," Cody breathed. "I guess you lucked out, Hackett."

"Are you kidding?" I said. "This is part of my punishment. She'll get me back tomorrow. Probably by giving me a D on my history project."

Cody tugged at my jacket. "C'mon. Geneva's waiting."

When we got outside, we spotted Geneva's little red pickup truck parked near the corner. About a trillion bumper stickers were plastered all over it. They said things like A CHANT EVERY DAY KEEPS THE WARMONGERS AWAY and CRYSTAL POWER and I AM A NUCLEAR-FREE ZONE. There was a smiling Buddha nodding in the back window.

Beads and crystals dripped off the rearview mirror.

We opened the door and slid inside. Geneva had her eyes closed, as if she were sleeping.

"Sorry we're late," Cody said.

Geneva held up a finger. Her long reddish-blond hair swayed in the breeze. She took several deep, slow breaths. Then her eyes popped open. "No problem," she said. "I always meditate while I'm waiting. When you're in touch with your inner self, you don't get antsy."

"Cool," I said. I rolled my eyes at Cody.

Geneva started the truck. "It's a fabulous day for a drive," she said as she pulled out on Bay Street. "Thank you, Mother Earth!" she yelled out the window. The guy in the next car gave her a weird look. Geneva smiled sunnily at him.

Here's the thing about Geneva. She might be a major flake, but she doesn't ask the typical dumb questions most older people do. You'll notice she didn't say, "How was school today?" Of course, she'll drive you bats talking about Mars and how it's somersaulting through the cosmos or something, but at least it's not boring. Wacky, maybe. But usually not too dull.

We drove down the coast highway, listening to Geneva talk about the power of the spring equinox and the best brand of tofu dogs.

When we got to St. Jude, we really had to hunt for a parking spot. The Smoked Oyster Festival had been that weekend, and there were still tourists around. Finally Geneva found a tiny alley we'd never noticed before and squeezed the truck into a space behind a Dumpster.

Cody took about an hour to pick out his bike. Then Geneva bought us pizza. We each had two slices, followed by ice cream for dessert.

So we were all pretty content as we strolled back to the car. I figured I even had time to make a dent in my assignments before dinner. That's when Geneva spotted the store.

We were walking down the tiny alley, finishing the rest of our cones. Geneva tossed her empty cup in the Dumpster.

"Hey," she said, "look at that."

Just beyond the Dumpster was a small shop. There was no name on the door, but the window display was cluttered with beads and crystals and drippy scarves like Geneva wore. Heaps of bracelets and rings were scattered on a gold velvet fringed shawl.

"Look at that shawl!" Geneva said. "It would look awesome with my purple dress. Really retro."

Cody and I sighed. When it came to teenage girls, it was always a shaky situation. One minute they're buying you pizza, and the next minute they're accessorizing.

"Look at that material," Geneva said.

"It's *you*," Cody said.

"But is velvet really *in* this year?" I asked, giving Cody a look.

Geneva grinned. "Can the act, wise guys. Let's go in. Look, they sell incense."

"Aw, come on, Geneva," Cody complained. "You'll be in there for hours."

"Minutes," Geneva said. "Promise."

Cody peered inside the shop window. "It looks pretty spooky to me. Dusty."

"And dark," I said. "Everything looks about a million years old." Cody was right, I thought with a shiver. The shop *did* look spooky.

Suddenly, the door swung open. There was nobody standing in the doorway, though. A cold breeze roared up the alley and swirled around our ankles.

"You may enter," a voice said.

"Awesome," Geneva breathed. "Come on!"

She disappeared inside the shop. Cody and I traded a glance. He shrugged. I shrugged. Neither one of us would admit that he was a little spooked about going in. So we went in.

Dark shadows loomed in every corner. An older woman with the blackest hair I'd ever seen sat behind the counter. Even all the way across the cluttered shop, her eyes glittered. Maybe it was because they caught the light of the only lamp in the place. Behind her, the shelves were filled with glass jars containing weird, darkish things.

"How did the door open like that?" Cody whispered to me.

The woman leaned over the counter. "Perhaps Fate opened the door," she said in a heavy accent.

"It was the wind. She's trying to scare you," I whispered to Cody.

"It's working," Cody whispered back.

Geneva pawed through the items in a woven basket. She held up a pair of earrings shaped like little bells.

"How much are these earrings?" Geneva's bright voice seemed to chase away some of the gloom of the shop.

"Fourteen ninety-five," the woman said.

Geneva made a face. "How about that shawl in the window? Does it come in any other colors?"

"C'mon," I said to Cody. "Let's look around. Geneva's going to take forever. I can feel it."

Cody and I poked around the old shop. It had great things, if you like stuffed reptile heads.

Everything was dusty and jumbled together. Weird looking wooden statues. Candles. Crystals. Beads. Bracelets. Books. Stuffed animals that looked like toys, except for their faces. If a little kid saw them, he'd run for cover.

Cody stayed near the front door. I guess he was still kind of creeped out. But I kept moving toward the back of the shop.

There was a dusty velvet curtain hanging over a doorway at the back of the shop. The cloth might have been red once, but now it was the color of dried blood. I tried to peek behind it without touching anything. It looked as though it led to a storage room that wasn't open to the public.

But a strange feeling came over me. I had to know what was back there.

I glanced behind me. Geneva had totally captured the old woman's attention. She had wrapped the gold shawl around her and was trying to match a necklace to it. I pushed aside the curtain and went in.

There wasn't much to see. A small round table had a teapot and one cup sitting on it. One wall was hung with pictures and rugs. A cabinet with glass doors stood against the other wall. It was so tall it reached the ceiling and looked like it might fall over any second.

But somehow I found myself standing in front of the cabinet. Dolls were arranged on the shelves. They were all shapes and sizes and colors. They had porcelain heads and fabric-stuffed bodies with jointed arms and legs.

But these didn't look like a little girl's dolls. There was something about the expression on their faces that was almost...human. Their strange glass eyes seemed to stare at me in a way that made my flesh creep.

"I'm outta here," I muttered, backing up.

But suddenly, I stopped. A doll on the third shelf had caught my eye. My feet seemed glued to the floor. I couldn't move. I stared at the doll, fascinated.

And as I stared, it was almost as though the doll started to talk to me. Only it didn't use words. It was more like a feeling. A call.

Slowly, I reached out and opened the door of the cabinet. My fingers closed around the doll. When they did, I felt a shock, like static electricity.

But it was funny. The doll seemed...warm. And it was chilly inside the shop.

I looked into the doll's glassy black eyes. I felt a little dizzy. *Sugar overload,* Geneva would say. *All that ice cream...*

But it wasn't sugar. I stumbled back against

the table. The doll slipped from my fingers, but I quickly caught it. It stared up at me accusingly...

That was it! The doll looked just like Mrs. Fink!

It had the same little beady eyes. The same skinny face. The same mouth turned down at the corners. No wonder I thought the doll had been calling me!

I tucked it under my arm and slipped past the curtain again. Cody was sitting on a footstool, his chin in his hands. He looked bored.

"Look what I found," I said in a quiet voice. I held the doll in front of him.

"Nice dolly," Cody said sarcastically.

"Look closer," I said. "Remind you of anyone?"

"No," Cody said. "But now that you mention it, it gives me the creeps."

"It's Mrs. Fink!" I said. "Can't you tell? It looks just like her."

"It does not," Cody said. "Get that thing away from me, Hackett."

I turned the doll's face back to me. "Don't you see it? It's *her*," I said.

"You've got El Finko on the brain," Cody said. "Come on, I think Geneva is done buying out the place. Let's split."

I trailed after Cody to the cash register. I knew I should put the doll down, but I couldn't. Something was telling me to buy it. I marched up to the counter, where the old woman was giving Geneva her change.

"How much for the doll?" I asked.

The woman took a step back. She made some sort of sign in the air. "Where did you get that? You were snooping!"

"I didn't mean to snoop," I said. "I thought the back of the shop was open. I want to buy the doll." I turned to Cody and Geneva. "It's for Annabel."

Geneva gave the doll a doubtful look. "Are you sure, Jesse? It's not very...uh, pretty."

"She'll love it," I said.

"The doll is not for sale," the woman said.

"But—"

"Not for sale!" the woman hissed. She snatched the doll out of my hands.

"Hey!" Geneva said. "There's no need to be rude."

"I think there is," the woman said. "This boy was trespassing. He took something he shouldn't have."

"He wants to buy it," Geneva said. "He wasn't *stealing*."

"I want it," I said.

"How much?" Geneva said. "The doll is in the shop. Therefore, it's for sale."

Geneva was a true mall rat. She knew her shopping rights.

"I tell you, no!" the woman said. "It is from my private collection."

"Well, would you consider selling it?" Geneva asked. She gave the woman a sunny smile. "It would be a shame if I told all my friends how *unfriendly* this shop is."

The woman looked from me to Geneva. Her lip curled. "You want it so badly?"

Geneva tossed her hair. "Obviously!"

I nodded. I didn't know *why* I wanted it so badly. I just knew I *did*. Suddenly, I wished I didn't want it at all. Suddenly, I was kind of hoping Geneva would shut up.

But the woman thrust the doll at me. It seemed to leap from her hands to mine. I caught it against my chest.

"Then take it!" she shrilled. "Take it and go."

"But how much—" Geneva said.

"It is my gift to you," the woman sneered. "Because the boy insisted."

The woman looked so mean that Geneva and I took a step backward. We wheeled around and hurried out of the shop. Cody was way ahead of us.

"And you, boy!" the woman called after me. "When the Shadow Zone darkens your door and chills your dreaming nights, do not return to me for help!"

A cold shiver ran down my spine as I crossed the threshold of the shop. And then the door slammed shut behind us.

All by itself.

4

When You Do Voodoo

When I got home, I put the doll in my closet so that Annabel wouldn't see it. She'd probably want to give it a bath or something. Not to mention that I didn't want to explain to Mom and Dad why I had a doll.

But there was something else. Somehow, I didn't want to look at the doll. I wanted it hidden away.

After dinner I told Dad I had a super amount of homework to do. But when I got upstairs, I just sat at my desk. Should I tackle the history paper? Or should I do the punishment first? I tried to decide which was more important. Which one would I get in more trouble for not doing?

I decided to do my punishment first. It was easy, and I wouldn't have to concentrate. I got out a clean sheet of paper and started to copy the Facts to Remember at the end of the chapter.

There were sixteen "facts," and each one was explained in three long paragraphs. This would take all night!

The good thing was that I didn't have to concentrate. The bad thing was that my thoughts could wander. And they wandered straight to the closet. I couldn't stop thinking about the doll. Mostly I couldn't stop wondering why I had taken it. What was I going to do with it now?

Finally, I threw down my pen and went to the closet. I got out the doll and propped it on my dresser.

It sat there, staring at me. Cody was right. It *was* weird. There was something almost human about it. Annabel pretended that her dolls were real all the time. But when I imagined pretending that this doll was real, I got a cold shiver. It would be like having a second Mrs. Fink!

That's when I got the idea. I sneaked into Annabel's room and took one of her doll dresses. It was a flowered number with a lace collar. Then I got some powder from the bathroom and dumped it on the doll's black hair. Now it looked gray. I pinched it up with a rubber band so it looked like a bun.

Pretty close. I just needed one more touch. I got some wire from Dad's toolbox and twisted it into a pair of spectacles. Then I placed them on the doll's nose.

When I stepped back to look, I let out a yelp. It was the spitting image of Mrs. Fink!

I'd just read this cool book called *Doctor Death*. In it, the terrible Dr. Zaxar practices voodoo magic. One of the ways he foils his enemies is to make dolls that look like them and then stick pins in them. The enemies would have heart attacks and fall down cliffs and stuff. It was awesome.

I chuckled to myself as I got a package of straight pins from Mom's sewing kit. I hurried back to my room and took a pin out. I stuck it in the doll's right arm.

Maybe Mrs. Fink wouldn't be able to grade papers. Ha,ha.

Then I went back to Facts to Remember. But the whole time I could feel the doll's eyes boring into me. I put it in the desk drawer. Maybe it was silly, but I breathed easier just the same.

I woke up on time, for once. The first thing I did was go to the drawer and peek in at the doll. I held her up. She still looked like Mrs. Fink. In the bright sunlight her eyes seemed lighter. Now they were close to Mrs. Fink's steel-gray color. I put the doll back and closed the drawer again.

I stuffed my homework and the few notes I'd taken into my binder. I'd read an account of the assassination of Abraham Lincoln and quickly wrote out some of the facts before I fell asleep. It wasn't much of a paper. If Mrs. Fink called on me, I'd just have to wing it.

It was another typical morning. Annabel couldn't find any clean socks, and Dad figured out that I'd forgotten to do the laundry. Mom heard that the first soft-shell crabs were in and she took off like a shot. Annabel threw a fit when there were no cookies for her lunch. Maybe I shouldn't have polished off the Fig Newtons while I was studying.

Cody was waiting for me at the end of his driveway. "Did you do the paper?" he asked.

"Sort of," I said. "Maybe I should get a really bad stomachache in the middle of class. I can go to the nurse."

"Mrs. Fink will know you're faking," Cody said. "She always does."

I almost told Cody right then that Mrs. Fink might have to run to the nurse herself. He might get a kick out of what I'd done. But something stopped me. Somehow, I wasn't sure if Cody would think it was funny.

Come to think of it, *I* wasn't sure if it was that funny, either.

The class was buzzing. Nobody knew what to make of it.

For the first time in the memory of Cape Sorrow Middle School, Mrs. Fink was late!

"Maybe she's sick," Burt Mackinac said.

"Maybe she's *dead,*" Joey Bartunek said.

And maybe I'd lucked out. Maybe I wouldn't have to read my paper after all.

But at five minutes after the bell, the door slowly creaked open. Mrs. Fink walked in.

I dropped my books with a crash. I didn't even bend down to get them. I just sat there, staring in shock.

Mrs. Fink's right arm was in a sling!

5

Black Magic

Coincidence! It just had to be. But it was a weird enough coincidence to shake me up.

"What happened, Mrs. Fink?" Debbi Oleander asked.

"I sprained my wrist," Mrs. Fink explained. "The good news is, it's not a bad sprain. The bad news is, I had to go to the emergency room. I couldn't grade your projects last night."

This was *bad* news?

"And you know what I always tell you," Mrs. Fink said. "If you get behind, catch up right away! So instead of continuing with the history papers today, I'd like to teach a regular lesson. That way I'll be able to grade your papers tonight and get caught up."

Saved! I blew out a breath of relief. I had another night to work on my paper. Not that it was enough time to net an A. But at least it would save me from complete humiliation.

Still, I felt guilty when I looked at Mrs. Fink's sling. I couldn't take my eyes off it. *It's not my fault,* I told myself. Sticking a pin in a doll couldn't really do anything.

Could it?

After school, Cody wanted to shoot some hoops, but I lied and told him I had to pick up Annabel. I could tell he thought something was wrong, but I couldn't explain that I was spooked. Cody just wouldn't get it.

Cody was a totally down-to-earth guy. While I read adventure stories, Cody devoured wood-working manuals. He was the only kid in town who didn't believe that there was buried trea-sure on Scull Island. On a campout, when the guys were telling ghost stories, Cody usually fell asleep right in the middle. He just didn't believe in things he couldn't see.

So I wasn't about to tell him that I was afraid I'd sprained Mrs. Fink's arm because I'd stuck a pin in a doll.

As soon as I got home, I pounded up the stairs and yanked open the drawer.

The doll stared up at me. I picked it up gin-gerly. There was a dark patch on one cheek that I hadn't noticed before. I guessed it was mildew. But it was right where Mrs. Fink's mole was!

"Don't weird out on me, Hackett," I muttered to myself.

But I had to be sure. I took the pin out of the doll's right arm. This time, I just *poked* the left arm; I didn't leave the pin in. If something weird was going on—and it *wasn't*—I didn't want to be responsible for breaking Mrs. Fink's arm. But I needed to give the doll a little test.

"Jesse?" Mom poked her head in the door. I quickly stood in front of the doll so she wouldn't see it. "I'm glad you're home," she said in a low voice.

Dad slept in the afternoons, so we went around whispering. The second floor was only for reading. If Annabel and I wanted to play a game, we had to go downstairs.

"I just brought Annabel home," Mom said. "Now I have to get to the restaurant and clean shrimp. Can you keep an eye on her?"

"Sure," I said.

"How was school today?" Mom asked.

"The usual," I said. *Hah!*

But Mom wasn't really listening. She was already thinking about all those shrimp she had to devein. "Love you," she said, and disappeared.

Annabel was playing quietly in her room, so I went downstairs and took out some chicken to defrost. Dad was making chicken parmigiana with spaghetti tonight. It was my favorite meal. Maybe it would take my mind off the strange stuff I was imagining.

It would probably have been an excellent idea to work on my paper. Not to mention that I still had that load of laundry to do. But I decided that an hour of TV wouldn't hurt.

I was crossing to the den when I heard a bump from upstairs. I heard Annabel humming. Then another bump.

Bump?

I ran out into the hall. Annabel was dreamily coming downstairs. She held the Mrs. Fink doll by one foot. Every time she hit another stair, the doll's head bumped against the step behind. *Bump!*

She was smashing Mrs. Fink's head to smithereens!

"Stop!" I screamed. I leaped up the stairs and tore the doll out of Annabel's hand. "Don't ever, *ever* touch this doll again!" I yelled.

Annabel burst into tears. "B—but I let you play with *my* dolls," she blubbered.

"I never play with your dolls," I said.

"But you *could*," Annabel said tearfully. She sniffed. "Because I'm not a mean, selfish brother who hogs his toys!"

"What's going on down there?" Dad asked. He stood at the top of the stairs. His sandy hair stuck straight up on one side, and his face was creased from the pillow. "Is everyone in one piece?"

"Sorry, Dad," I said. I gave Annabel a warning look. She hiccuped, but she didn't cry again. "Go back to sleep," I said. "It's only four o'clock."

Dad disappeared back into the bedroom.

"Why do you have a doll, Jesse?" Annabel whispered to me. "You don't like dolls."

"This is a special doll," I said. I took her hand and led her down the stairs. "It's very expensive. And you can't play with it, okay?"

Annabel nodded. "Can I look at it?"

"Only if you ask me first," I said. I rummaged in the cupboard and came up with a bag of oat-meal cookies. "If you promise to be good, you can have a cookie before supper. Okay?"

"I promise," Annabel said, reaching for the cookie.

I left Annabel in front of the TV and hurried upstairs with the doll. I hid it on the top shelf of my closet, beyond Annabel's reach.

Even though the closet was dark, the gray eyes seemed to glow at me. Was her mouth the same as before? Now it seemed to curve upward a bit at the corners. As though the doll was trying not to smile...

"Nah," I said, and closed the closet door.

Dad ended up oversleeping, which meant that dinner was late. Which meant that I didn't get to my books until almost eight o'clock. I found some background detail on John Wilkes Booth and called it a night.

So I wasn't exactly looking forward to school the next day. I didn't know what would be worse—something happening to Mrs. Fink, or something *not* happening.

I was quiet on the way to school. Cody didn't seem to notice. He was too busy complaining that his mom wouldn't let him ride his new bike until his birthday on Saturday.

"I mean, I've *seen* it," Cody said as we entered the schoolyard. "What's the big surprise? It's green and has two wheels."

I stopped paying attention. Kids were laughing and joking and pushing each other around. Burt Mackinac was tossing a football back and forth with a couple of other guys. Everything looked perfectly normal. But where was Mrs. Fink?

Then I saw her. She was talking to Ms. Macro,

the English teacher. Mrs. Fink's right arm was still in a sling, but she looked perfectly fine. As I watched, she turned away and started toward the school entrance.

Relief trickled through me like a long sip of cold lemonade on a hot day. She was okay. My imagination was in overdrive, as usual.

But just then, Burt Mackinac threw a spinning pass to Andy Reiser. Only Andy had turned away to talk to Joey Bartunek.

The football slammed into Mrs. Fink's left arm! Her books and big purse went flying as she lost her balance. She fell backward, hitting her head on the edge of one of the stone stairs to the school entrance.

She was out cold!

6

Jaws

Ms. Macro screamed and rushed toward Mrs. Fink. A hush fell over the schoolyard as Mr. Callas, the gym teacher, ran into the school building.

After a few minutes, the principal, Mrs. Tolkin, came out, clapped her hands and told all the homeroom teachers to bring their classes inside. Ms. Macro took over our class. As we walked inside, we heard the wail of the ambulance.

"I guess you lucked out again," Cody whispered to me. "But Mrs. Fink sure didn't."

"Luck had nothing to do with it," I said.

"What do you mean?" Cody asked.

"That was no accident," I said, shivering.

"You mean Burt *meant* to hit Mrs. Fink?" Cody asked. His freckles smashed together as he wrinkled his nose doubtfully.

I shook my head. "That's not what I mean," I said. "It was—"

Ms. Macro rapped on the desk. "Class! Be quiet." But just then we heard the ambulance pull into the schoolyard. Everyone ran to the windows, including Ms. Macro.

Mrs. Fink was loaded onto a stretcher and rolled into the ambulance. Her eyes were still closed and her face was paper white. After a minute, the ambulance sped away.

"All right, class," Ms. Macro said shakily. "Everyone take their seats. Now, if you'll all open your history books..."

I opened my book, but I couldn't make sense of the page. The letters blurred and leaped around. Mrs. Fink was unconscious. Maybe even dying. And it was all my fault!

Nobody was more relieved than I when the last bell rang. I picked up my knapsack. Cody waved good-bye to me across the room. Today he was stopping at the library. I was just as glad not to have to walk home with him.

It had started to rain during last period, so I opened my knapsack to get my sweatshirt. When I took it out and unrolled it, the doll fell out!

I choked back a scream. What was it doing in my knapsack? Could Annabel have put it there?

I started to reach down for it, but suddenly, a hand snatched it away.

"Whoa, look at this," Joey Bartunek said.

Great. If there was one guy in the entire sixth grade who shouldn't see a doll fall out of a guy's knapsack, it was loudmouth Joey Bartunek.

"Hey, give that back," I said.

But it was too late.

"Whoa," Joey crowed, "look what Hackett brought to school today. His dol–ly," he sang out.

I looked around. Luckily, no one was paying attention. Everyone was filing out. When it comes to the last bell, kids don't fool around.

"Did you miss your dolly-wolly, Hackett?" Joey crooned. "Whoa, don't ask me why. This face could stop a truck."

"Can it, Bartunek," I snarled. "It's my sister's."

I reached for the doll, but Joey held it just out of my reach.

"Whatsa matter?" he said, his little eyes shining like green pebbles. "Are you going to cry without your dolly? Boo hoo, little Jesse lost his—*Yeeeeooowww!*"

Suddenly, Joey dropped the doll on the floor. He held up his hand. A strange look came over his face. "Hey," he said, "that doll *bit* me!"

I quickly snatched it back and stuffed it into my pack. "Yeah, right, Bartunek," I said. Joey had probably gotten his finger caught on a sharp edge of the wire glasses. Because even voodoo dolls can't bite. No way.

Joey looked down at his hand and back up at me. His face was awfully pale. "Weird doll, Hackett," he muttered.

"Aw, did the dolly-wolly bite you?" I asked. I couldn't resist. "Boo hoo!"

But Joey didn't rise to the bait. He backed away from me, straight into the trash can. It fell over with a clang. He sprinted for the door.

I couldn't help chuckling as I tugged on my sweatshirt and pulled the hood over my head. At least the doll was good for *something*.

When I got home, the house was dark and quiet. Rain drummed on the roof, and thunder rolled across the sky. There was a note on the refrigerator from Mom:

Annabel and I went shopping for new shoes. Dad's still asleep. Try to get some schoolwork done while it's quiet. Remember, tonight's restaurant night. Love you, Mom.

Every Thursday was restaurant night. We ate at the Blue Bay Cafe so that we could spend time with Mom. She usually managed to sit down with us for about five minutes before she had to run away to blacken some catfish or something.

I went up to my room and tossed the knapsack on the desk. Lightning split the sky, and I jumped. The knapsack sat there, like it was mocking me. I had to get rid of the doll. But what if it was true—that I'd really created a voodoo doll? Whatever I did to it might happen to Mrs. Fink. What if I tossed it in Menhaden Bay and Mrs. Fink ended up drowning in her bathtub?

What had that weird lady at the shop said— that the *Shadow Zone* would be darkening my door?

"The Shadow Zone," I whispered. Rain lashed against the windowpane, and I shivered. Just saying the words out loud seemed to chill the air.

But suddenly, the air felt more than cold. It was like ice.

Because the buckle to my knapsack was moving. *All by itself.*

The flap opened. A small arm poked out. Lightning flashed as the head of the doll swiveled toward me and blinked its glassy gray eyes.

"Hello, Mr. Hackett," the doll said. "We meet at last!"

7

No Way Out

I couldn't move. I couldn't talk. I could only watch as the doll's head swiveled around to examine the bedroom.

"Phew," it said. "I can finally breathe. It's musty in there. And don't you ever throw out those old candy wrappers?"

"Who—who—who—" I stammered.

"You sound like an owl," the doll said.

The eyes blinked again. The doll looked more like Mrs. Fink than ever. The dark patch was definitely a mole. And it was the shape of Brazil!

"Stop staring," the doll snapped. "Mind your manners."

"I'm dreaming," I babbled. "This is the biggest, baddest nightmare I've ever had."

The doll suddenly leaped off the desk and landed on the floor. She walked stiffly over to the bed. Then she pinched my leg.

"Ow!" I said.

"You seem awake to me," she said. The eyes blinked shut once, twice. It made my skin crawl.

"Now compose yourself," the doll said. "We have things to do. I'd say clean out your knapsack, for starters."

"Who—*what*—are you?" I breathed. "Are you Mrs. Fink?"

"Close, but no cigar," the doll said. "Let's just say that it's thanks to her—and you—that I'm here. Don't worry about the details."

"Wait a sec—" I started.

"Don't interrupt!" the doll barked. "Lesson Number One: I'm the boss here, buster. I know you're not very good at lessons, but can you try to remember that one?"

A loud crack of thunder made me jump. That's when I realized that my muscles could actually function. So I did what any normal guy would do. I ran.

I leaped through the doorway, pounded down the stairs, and raced out the front door. The cold rain lashed at my face, but I didn't stop running until I got to Cody's house. If ever I needed a friend, it was now. Because I was either crazy or in major trouble. I banged on the door.

Cody opened it. He peered at me. "What's wrong with you?"

"You've got to come home with me," I said.

"I was just starting my homework," Cody said, frowning. He hated to have his schedule upset.

I grabbed his arm. "This is a life-or-death situation, Cody. You have to come. *Now.*"

"What—"

"I can't tell you," I said. "You won't believe me. I have to *show* you."

Still grumbling, Cody grabbed his jacket. We sloshed through puddles as we ran back to my house.

When we got there, I pounded up the stairs, Cody at my heels. We burst into my room together.

The doll was now sitting on the desk. Her glassy gray eyes stared straight ahead.

"Look," I panted.

"At what?" Cody said impatiently.

"The doll," I whispered.

"Whoa," Cody said, "hold the phone. Are you telling me that you dragged me over here in the pouring rain to look at a *doll?*"

"It's not just a doll," I said.

"I know," Cody said. "It's that stupid doll you got at that shop." He walked a little closer to examine it. "So you dressed it up like Mrs. Fink. So what?"

"So listen," I said. I took a deep breath. "It talked to me," I whispered. "And it *moved*."

Cody rolled his eyes. "And I can fly."

I went over and poked the doll. I moved one arm up and down. "C'mon," I said. "You wouldn't shut up before. Talk! Move!"

"Jesse, give me a break," Cody said. He was starting to sound annoyed. "Enough already."

"Look at it!" I said. "Its eyes are gray now. They were black before. Remember? And look— it even has the mole right where Mrs. Fink's is! And it's shaped like Brazil!"

"Yeah," Cody said. "You did a really good job of drawing it."

"I didn't draw it!" I exclaimed. "All I did was make the glasses and put some powder into the hair. But look—" I rubbed my hands in the doll's creepy hair. I shuddered. The hair felt so... *human.*

"There's no powder anymore," I said to Cody. "The hair turned gray, all by itself. And then, when I stuck a pin in the doll's arm, Mrs. Fink sprained her wrist. And after Annabel bumped the doll down the stairs, Mrs. Fink hit her head! That's not just a coincidence, Cody!"

Cody shook his head in disgust. "This is just like the time you tried to convince me that there was a gigantic sea monster out by Scull Island. I didn't believe you then, either."

It was true. When we were younger, I used to concoct wild stories and try to get Cody to believe them. Why hadn't I kept my mouth shut?

"It's not a trick, Cody," I said desperately.

I pulled at the doll's legs and tried to make it walk. I opened the doll's mouth, trying to make it talk. "I'm telling you, this doll is alive!" I cried, holding the doll out toward him.

"Get that thing away from me!" Cody said, swatting it. "Do you think I'm stupid or something?"

Just then, I felt the doll's hand tighten around my wrist. "Yes!" I yelled.

Cody froze. His face was bright red. "You think I'm stupid," he repeated. "I knew it. Just because I have to study to get good grades. Just because I don't have any imagination—"

"Cody, I didn't—" I started. But just then my door creaked open. Annabel poked her head around it.

"Mom said to tell you that we're home," she said. Her dark eyes grew round when she saw the doll. "Can I play, too?"

"Great," Cody said to me, "now it's going to be all over the neighborhood that we're playing with dolls. Thanks a bunch, Hackett. Talk about stupid moves!"

Cody stalked out. I pushed Annabel out of the room, shut the door, and followed him downstairs. He said a polite hello to my mom and stomped off toward the front door, his sneakers squishing.

I wanted to run after him, but I couldn't leave. What if Annabel went back into my room to play with the doll? I'd have to apologize to Cody at school tomorrow.

I turned on my heel and raced back upstairs. I heard Annabel humming in her room and peeked inside.

Annabel had the Mrs. Fink doll!

"What are you doing?" I shouted. "I told you never to touch that doll!"

Annabel gazed at me defiantly. "But you left her in my room!"

"I did not!" I said. The doll couldn't have opened the door of my room. Could it? I stared at the doll, horrified.

"She looked sick," Annabel said, gazing fondly at the doll. "I gave her TLC—tender loving care. See?" She held up the doll. The goony kid had put a bandage on the doll's forehead and wrapped her arm in toilet paper.

"All better," Annabel cooed. She cradled the doll in her arms and rocked it soothingly.

Slowly, the doll's left eye closed in a wink.

Something snapped inside me. I crossed the room in two bounds and snatched the doll out of Annabel's arms. I had to get rid of it. Now. Today.

I leaned in close to Annabel's face and spoke in my scariest big-brother voice. "If you lay *one* little finger on this doll, Annabel Hackett, I'll take all of your dolls away. And I'll throw them into Menhaden Bay and drown them!"

"You're mean!" Annabel cried. "You're mean and I hate you, Jesse!"

"What is going on, you two?" Dad said, appearing in the doorway. "Are you trying to drive me crazy or just insane?"

"Sorry, Dad," I said.

"Jesse's mean," Annabel sobbed.

Dad went over and picked Annabel up. "What's the matter, sweetheart?" he said.

"He's going to drown my dolls," Annabel said, sniffing. She gave me a triumphant look. *Gotcha!* it said.

But I didn't care if she got me in trouble. I just had to keep her away from the doll.

Dad shot me a warning look. "It's okay, sweetie pie," he said to Annabel. "Jesse won't drown your dolls. And if he *does*, I'll save them. And Jess, what did you do to the laundry? All my T-shirts are pink."

When I finally did the laundry yesterday, I'd forgotten to separate the colors from the whites. Annabel's new red dress had run.

I must have looked pretty guilty, because Dad just laughed. "It's okay," he said. "I just hope the guys at work don't tease me. Now, are you guys ready? It's time to meet Mom."

"I just need one second," I said.

I carried the doll downstairs and dashed outside in the rain. I opened up the garbage can and stuffed the doll inside. Then I replaced the lid.

The garbagemen would pick it up tomorrow morning. It would get thrown in the truck and end up in some landfill somewhere. It wouldn't be my problem anymore.

When we got home from dinner, Annabel was half asleep. I made sure she got into her pajamas and brushed her teeth while Dad got ready for work.

Then I sat with her on the edge of her bed while she placed her favorite stuffed animals around her.

"You wouldn't drown Boris, would you?" she asked me sleepily.

Boris was her fuzzy black bear. "No," I said, "I'd never drown Boris."

Annabel's eyelids fluttered closed. I went back to my room and opened my closet door to get my pajamas.

And there it was. I stumbled backward in horror.

The Mrs. Fink doll was sitting on the top shelf again! "Sweet dreams," she said.

I buried my face in my hands and rocked back and forth. I'd never get rid of it. There was no way out.

8

Oh, You Horrible Doll

I woke up the next morning with a crick in my neck. Boy, was I glad to see daylight. I'd had the worst nightmares.

I'd dreamt that Mrs. Fink had been here, making me straighten all the shoes in my closet. Then I'd cleaned out the gunk in my knapsack. After that, I refolded my sweaters and T-shirts. And finally, I had to organize the papers on my desk.

And *then,* at long last, when I was so exhausted that I couldn't even stand up any more, she made me sleep on the floor while *she* took the bed!

I yawned sleepily. What an awesomely terrible dream!

I screamed as the Mrs. Fink doll's head popped over the edge of the bed and looked down at me.

"Rise and shine!" she hissed, right in my face.

"Let's wash up! You have time for twenty minutes of studying before school!"

I moaned out loud.

"Jesse? Are you all right?" The door opened and Dad poked his head around the corner.

"What are you doing on the floor?"

"I—I fell out of bed," I said, getting to my feet. "I guess I had a nightmare."

More than anything, I wanted to tell Dad what was going on. But the doll wouldn't perform for Cody, so it was a good bet that it wouldn't even move an eyelash in front of my dad. It was bad enough that Cody thought I was trying to play a joke on him. Dad would probably book me a padded cell.

The Mrs. Fink doll was lying in the middle of my bed. Dad picked it up. "What are you doing with Annabel's doll? Didn't this cause all that commotion yesterday?"

"Uh," I said, stalling.

Dad sighed. "I wish you wouldn't provoke your sister, Jesse. You're really getting too old for it."

"You're absolutely right, Dad," I said. "I'll take the doll back to her and apologize."

"Good," Dad said. "Then come downstairs. I'm making fried-egg sandwiches." He tossed the doll toward me. A small cry escaped the doll as it flew through the air. I caught it and clamped it to my chest.

Dad looked startled. "Wow. Amazing technology they have these days. That sounded real. *Too* real," he muttered, turning away. "I wonder how Annabel can sleep with that thing in the room."

"I know exactly what you mean," I said.

Cody wasn't waiting at the end of his driveway for me, so I figured he was still mad. I trudged to school, wondering how many more ways the doll could ruin my life.

I'd been too scared to leave the doll in the house while Dad was sleeping. I pictured it leaping onto his chest and biting his nose. It scared me even more to shove it in my knapsack and take it to school. But I did. I figured I could stash it in my locker. Even a voodoo doll couldn't manage to get out of a locker with a combination lock, could it?

At least I wouldn't have to worry about Mrs. Fink and my history paper. After that clunk on the head, she'd probably be out for weeks.

But when I pushed open the door, I bumped straight into Mrs. Fink!

"Good morning, Jesse," she said.

"Mrs. Fink! It's you!"

"Apparently," she said.

"But the ambulance took you away," I said.

"I was unconscious," Mrs. Fink said. "But the doctors checked me out, and I'm fine. I feel much better today. Even my wrist feels better."

"That's super," I gulped. I wouldn't say Mrs. Fink was *looking* better, though. There were circles under her eyes. She looked like she hadn't slept in days.

"Which means I'm looking forward to hearing your history paper today," she said, giving me a meaningful look. She walked off toward the classroom.

I stared at her back as she disappeared down the hall. How had she gotten better so quickly?

TLC.

Annabel!

She'd bandaged the doll and rocked it and soothed it. Had Annabel made Mrs. Fink better? Cody appeared at the end of the hall. He saw me, too, but he didn't wave. He walked toward his locker.

I hurried down the hall toward him. "Hey," I said, "what's up?"

"Not much," he said coolly. "Unless you want to introduce me to Frankenstein today. I just might be *stupid* enough to buy it."

"I didn't mean you were stupid yesterday," I

said. "When I said yes, I wasn't talking to you. I was *reacting*."

"Oh," Cody said. "To what?"

"The doll had just squeezed my arm," I explained.

Cody slammed his hand against his locker. "That's it!" he said. "You did it again!"

"Cody, just listen a second," I said. I twirled the lock on my locker and opened the door. "There really is something weird about this doll." I took it out of the knapsack and placed it on the high shelf in my locker.

"What's weird about it is that you brought it to school," Cody said.

"I'm afraid to leave it in the house," I said. "What if it bit my dad?"

Cody's face got so red that it matched his hair. "Why don't you just eat some paste, Jesse Hackett!"

Suddenly, a shadow loomed over Cody's shoulder. It was Mrs. Fink!

"Gentlemen? Would you mind telling me what all the shouting is about?"

I quickly slammed my locker door shut. Then I gave the answer any red-blooded American boy would give.

"Nothing," I said.

"We were just talking," Cody said.

Mrs. Fink raised an eyebrow. "Talking? The decibel level was about to raise the roof."

We shrugged.

And then Mrs. Fink turned to me. "What's in your locker, Mr. Hackett?"

I moved in front of it. "Books and stuff," I said nervously. "You know."

"Yes, Mr. Hackett, I *do* know, unfortunately." Mrs. Fink's lips pressed together, making them a thin line. "I remember the ferret incident."

Geez. Bring a ferret to school for one day, and you're marked for life. I never get a break.

"Open it," Mrs. Fink said. She rapped on the door.

"I forgot my combination," I said.

"That's what we were yelling about," Cody said. "I called him stupid." He turned to me. "I'm sorry I called you stupid, Jesse," he said in a really sincere voice. What an actor! "It was a totally mean and awful thing to say."

Mrs. Fink reached out a finger and flicked the open combination lock. "It's not locked. Open the door, Mr. Hackett. *Now.*"

What could I do? I opened the door. I looked at Mrs. Fink's face. I waited for her reaction to a truly ugly doll dressed just like her. I'd probably have detention for fifty years.

Mrs. Fink's face drained of color. She seemed

frozen to the spot as she stared at the doll. Then she took a shaky step backward.

But suddenly, the doll plunged off the shelf and flew at Mrs. Fink!

Mrs. Fink batted it away, and the doll landed on the floor, right on its head. I heard a sickening sound, like a pumpkin smashing. But the doll didn't break.

Mrs. Fink put a hand to her forehead. She stumbled.

"Mrs. Fink?" I whispered.

She started to fall. Mr. Callas, the gym teacher, was just coming down the hall. He caught her in his arms. Ms. DeBolt, the volleyball coach, was with him.

"She's unconscious again," he said. "You'd better call an ambulance."

I turned back to Cody. His freckles stood out against his pale face.

"I think she'll be okay," I said nervously.

Cody swallowed hard. He pointed to the floor.

"I saw it," he croaked. "It leaped off the shelf straight at her. I saw it! And, and—"

"What?" I said.

"Did you see its expression?" Cody breathed. He pointed down at the doll.

I looked down. The doll's mouth was now curved up at the corners. *Way* up.

"It's *smiling,*" Cody said.

Cody and I exchanged glances.

"Do you believe me now?" I whispered. I picked up the doll and threw it into the locker. I slammed the door shut and locked it.

Cody shivered. "I believe you. What are we going to do?"

"I've tried to get rid of it," I said. "I threw it in the garbage. It keeps coming back!"

"Can't you just return it?" Cody whispered.

Go back to that creepy shop and deal with that scary lady?

"Why didn't I think of that?" I said.

9

Getting Rid of Fink

The bus doors closed with a whoosh, nearly catching my shirttail. Cody and I hurried down the streets of St. Jude. This time, we remembered the way.

The narrow alley looked even darker and more sinister than I remembered. The knapsack thudded on my back as we ran. Cody and I had agreed not to say anything about our destination, in case the doll could hear us.

We skirted the Dumpster and stood in front of the shop. The front window was empty. The glass was caked with dirt and soot. Cobwebs dripped from the door frame. I tried the knob. Locked.

That's when Cody pointed to the sign hung high over our heads on the door.

CLOSED.

"It looks like no one has been here for *years*," Cody whispered.

We looked at each other in despair. What were we going to do?

When I got back to my room, I threw my backpack against the wall.

"Ow!"

"Oh, shut up," I said.

I watched as the backpack buckle slowly unfastened itself. The little arm popped out. Then the little face.

"I know you tried to get rid of me," the doll snarled, climbing out of my pack. The gray eyes blinked. The little arms crossed against her chest. "Don't you know yet that you can't?"

Hopelessness thudded through me. I sank down on the edge of my bed.

The doll walked toward me jerkily. Her words seemed to hit me like little fists. "You didn't choose me, Jesse. I chose you. I called you that day in the shop. And you listened. I told you to dress me up as the person you hate. And you did. You're in this with me, Jesse Hackett!"

"I'm *not* in this with you," I said dully. "I didn't want to hurt anybody."

The doll snorted. "Tell it to someone who doesn't know how bad you really are."

She hopped up on the bed next to me. "So,

partner," she said. "Now you have to do exactly what I say. First I want you to make a phone call. Think you can handle it?"

"No," I said. "I'm not doing *anything* for you. Things have gone far enough."

"I wouldn't say that," the doll said in a voice low with menace. "I'd say they haven't gone far enough. Doesn't your father sleep all afternoon? All *alone?*"

"You'd hurt my dad?" I breathed.

I heard the fiendish snapping of the doll's teeth. "Do you want to try me?"

I sprang off the bed. "Okay!" I cried. "I'll do what you want." I crept out into the hallway and brought the phone back into my room.

"Do you have the principal's number?" the doll asked.

"I guess," I said. I got Mom's phone book and looked under "School." Then I called Mrs. Tolkin.

"Give me the phone," the doll hissed. I put it up next to her mouth.

"Hello, Mrs. Tolkin? This is Mrs. Fink calling," the doll said. "Yes, the hospital released me."

She sounded exactly like Mrs. Fink!

"No, I'm sorry to say I'm not well, actually," the doll said. "It looks as though I'll need some time to rest. My nephew in Wyoming has offered to let me stay in his home for as long as I need to. Yes, of course..."

I gazed at the doll, horrified, as she thanked Mrs. Tolkin. Then she told me to hang up.

The doll turned to me. "It's time to vacuum that living room rug," she said briskly. "Annabel left crumbs all over it. Then you'll work on your history paper."

"But it's Friday night!" I protested.

"And it's due Monday," the doll replied.

"What really happened to Mrs. Fink?" I blurted. "Is she in the hospital? Is she..."

I stopped. I could hardly think the word, let alone say it: *Dead.*

The doll hopped down from the bed. "You wouldn't understand where she is. And why would you care?" She bared her teeth in an awful grin. "*I'm* the one you have to worry about now."

When I woke up the next morning, the Mrs. Fink doll told me that I was going to the library. "But it's Saturday!" I said.

The doll hopped up on my pillow and pulled my ear. "You should have gone to the library for research in the first place," she hissed. "You've been very lazy."

I tried to twist away, but that just made it

worse. "But I have to watch Annabel this morning," I protested.

"There's a children's story hour on Saturday mornings, isn't there?" the doll said. "You can leave Annabel there while you gather your research materials."

"How do you know about story hour?" I asked.

"Mrs. Fink knows it," the doll said. "She used to volunteer to read."

"To little kids?" I asked, surprised. "She must have scared them to death."

"Actually, she was pretty popular," the doll said. "Now get up. You have to do your chores before you go. Remember to put the wash in before you mow the lawn. That way, the clothes can be in the dryer while you clean your room."

"Okay, okay," I said.

"And you have just enough time to iron some T-shirts," the doll finished.

"Iron *T-shirts?*" I said in disbelief. "No way, José! Even Mrs. Fink wouldn't insist on ironed T-shirts."

The doll gave my ear a sharp yank. "Punishment," she hissed. "For trying to give me away."

"Do you blame me?" I said, putting a hand to my smarting ear.

"Oh, yes," the doll cooed. "Every day."

Dad was pretty puzzled at this new mania for ironing T-shirts. But I told him I wanted to look nice for Cody's birthday. I was supposed to go over to the Glimcher's for cake later in the afternoon.

I took Annabel to the library and left her happily listening to *The Bear Who Invented Breakfast.* And I have to admit that I found some totally cool books for my project. One described how Lincoln had lived for quite a while after being shot. I got some pretty gruesome details of his last hours.

It wasn't easy to concentrate with the doll in my knapsack. I kept expecting her to climb out and take a bite out of my foot. But as long as I was doing what she wanted, she left me alone.

I dropped Annabel off just in time for her to go to the movies with my parents. That meant I could safely leave the doll at home. I stuck her on the closet shelf.

She bared her teeth at me. "Be home by five, or else."

I slammed the closet door.

*   *   *

At the Glimcher's, Cody opened the door before I could even ring the bell.

"Any change?" he asked anxiously.

I told Cody how the doll had impersonated Mrs. Fink. "I don't know what really happened to her," I said. "The doll won't tell me."

Cody swallowed. "What does that mean? Is Mrs. Fink *dead?*"

"I don't know," I said. "I don't think so. The doll said I wouldn't understand. That doesn't sound like she's dead, does it?"

Cody just shrugged.

We slumped down on the living room couch. Things were worse than hopeless. No matter what I did, they just got worse.

"What if she *is* dead?" I whispered to Cody. "It will be all my fault!"

"Just relax," Cody said. Which was funny, since his leg was jumping about a hundred miles a minute. "The thing is, we can't handle this by ourselves. We don't know anything about voodoo and black magic and all that stuff."

"Right," I said. "But the shop is closed and the weird lady is gone. What are we going to do? March into the police station and say 'Help, my doll kidnapped my teacher'?"

"Of course not," Cody said. "But there has to

be *somebody* who can help us."

"I'm really scared, Cody," I said. "This is the worst thing that's ever happened to me."

Cody nodded. "Scarier than when I had my appendix out."

"Scarier than when our sailboat capsized, and my dad and I drifted on the bay for hours in the dark," I said.

"You wouldn't go sailing for months after that," Cody said, remembering.

I heard the faint sound of tiny bells, and Geneva drifted into the living room. She was wearing the earrings she'd bought in St. Jude.

"Jesse was right to listen to his inner voice," Geneva said. "Water is a very powerful force. If your energy field is a little whacked out, it's better to stay grounded."

As usual, Geneva summed everything up for us Earth dwellers.

"Right, Geneva," Cody said. "Let us know when you stop orbiting the planet."

"Scoff all you want, nonbeliever," Geneva said, "but there are deep, powerful forces out there."

Cody blew out an exasperated breath, but I sat up as the solution roared through my brain.

We *did* know someone who could help us. Someone who wouldn't rush us to a loony bin after she heard our story. Someone who could hear about walking, talking dolls and say "cool." Someone who knew about magic and spells and deep, powerful forces we didn't understand.

I cleared my throat. "Uh, Geneva? Can we talk?"

10

A Terrible Tumble

Geneva listened to me as I spilled out the story. She didn't even interrupt. A couple of times she nodded. Once she murmured, "Of course."

"So what do you think?" Cody asked when I was finally finished.

Geneva stared at the floor. She twisted a strand of red-gold hair around her finger. "Interesting," she murmured.

"Try terrifying," I said. "Do you really believe me, Geneva?"

"Of course," Geneva said. She lapsed into silence again.

"Geneva, come *on*," Cody urged. "Can you help us or are you just going to sit there meditating?"

Geneva gave Cody a cool look. "Since you're coming to me for help, do you really think it's a good idea to make fun of me?"

"Okay, I'm sorry," Cody said. "But can you help us?"

Geneva grinned. "Piece of cake."

"That's right," Mrs. Glimcher said, popping her head into the living room. "Come on, you guys. It's time for the birthday cake!"

Normally, it would have been a stellar afternoon. Mrs. Glimcher's chocolate cake was primo stuff. But Cody and I gobbled down our cake without tasting it. Cody tried on the cool sweatshirt Geneva had given him without really seeing it. We were all relieved when Mr. and Mrs. Glimcher said they'd clear up and we could clear out.

I looked at my watch as we hurried back to the living room. Four-thirty. I had to beat Mom and Dad back from the movies. And the doll had told me to return by five. Time was running out.

"Okay," Geneva said. "Here's what we have to do. First of all, I'll do some research on voodoo and try to figure out exactly what's happened."

Cody glanced at me, then asked, "Do you think Mrs. Fink is...dead?"

Geneva shook her head. "I doubt it. It sounds like the doll is using Mrs. Fink's energy to animate itself. So Mrs. Fink has to be alive."

"But where is she?" I asked.

Geneva thought a moment. "It probably depends on how much energy the doll has drained from Mrs. Fink," she said. "If Mrs. Fink is weak enough, the doll could have banished her to another dimension."

We were all quiet, thinking about what Geneva had said. Then Cody asked, "But why did the doll pick on Jesse?"

I already knew the answer to that one. *Because I was thinking evil thoughts. The doll saw my hate, and it chose me.*

Geneva shrugged. "I'd say he was in the wrong place at the wrong time. But that's not important. What we have to worry about is finding a way to control the doll. All this popping up when you least expect it isn't cool."

"You can say that again," I said, sneaking a glance at my watch.

"And then we have to get Mrs. Fink back," Geneva said. "If we can."

It sure didn't sound too promising. But it was better than nothing. I looked at my watch again.

"Go ahead home, Jesse," Geneva said. "Keep an eye on the doll. I'll get back to you."

When I got home, my parents and Annabel had just gotten back from the movies.

"I hope you left room for dinner," Mom said.

"Cold roast chicken and salad," Dad said. "And I'm going to make potatoes." He started off toward the kitchen.

"French fries!" Annabel said, hopping after him.

Mom came over and gave me a hug. "I wanted to tell you, Jesse, that I've noticed how hard you've been trying lately. Your room is clean and your chores get done. Not only that, I've never seen the laundry look so good. You're much better than your dad at folding!"

Actually, the doll had taught me how to fold. And she'd introduced me to bleach.

"You're the best," Mom murmured, kissing me.

"Thanks, Mom," I mumbled. Now I *really* felt guilty. I wasn't good because I was trying hard. I was good because a slave driver was forcing me.

"I'm going to grab a shower," Mom said. "Then I have to go back to the restaurant."

I followed Mom upstairs. It was five-fifteen. I was late.

The doll was waiting on the desk. "Where have you been?" she snapped.

"I have a life, you know," I said.

"A messy, disorganized one," the doll said. "Why did you stay at your friend's so long?"

I felt uneasy as that stare bored into me. "I

was eating cake. Opening presents. The usual birthday drill."

"Anything else?" the doll said. "You wouldn't be plotting anything, would you? Because that would be a very big mistake."

"I'm not plotting anything," I said nervously. I sat down at my desk. When I reached for a book, my hands were shaking. Was the doll psychic or something? "Now, do you mind? My history paper is due."

"Past due is more like it," the doll sneered. She hopped over and jumped up on the bed.

I started to read. "Don't forget to take notes!" the doll shrilled.

I forced myself to concentrate. Sure, a voodoo doll was on my back. But I still had to worry about flunking out.

It was weird, but this stuff was actually starting to be interesting. I usually daydreamed through Mrs. Fink's class. I skimmed the reading assignments and wrote the bare minimum on essay questions. But this Civil War stuff wasn't bad.

I was deep into the chapter "If Lincoln Had Lived" when Dad poked his head in my room.

"Did Mom go to work?" he asked.

"I don't think so," I said. "She was going to take a shower."

"What's that?" Dad asked.

I jumped. I thought maybe he was asking about the doll again. But he meant my book.

"It's a book on Lincoln," I said. "I'm doing a history paper on his assassination."

"On Saturday night?" Dad shook his head. "You really *are* changing, Jesse."

But suddenly I wasn't thinking about Lincoln anymore. I was looking past Dad's shoulder at the bed. A horrible feeling pierced through me.

Where was the doll?

I stood up so quickly I knocked over my desk chair.

"Jesse? You all right?"

"I—" I said.

But I didn't get a chance to finish. Suddenly, we heard a scream and a thumping noise.

Dad and I rushed out into the hall and toward the stairs. Mom was lying all twisted at the bottom.

"Eve!" Dad yelled. He started down the stairs toward her. I was right behind him.

But I stopped at the landing halfway down. The Mrs. Fink doll sat leaning against the bannister. Her blank gaze was pure evil.

The doll had pushed Mom down the stairs!

11

Desperate Measures

"Jesse!"

Dad's voice was frantic. The stairs seemed as if they were a long, dark tunnel. I met Dad's frightened eyes.

"Call 911!" he said.

I started back up the stairs toward the phone, but Mom stopped me.

"No," she said, "I'm okay. It's just my wrist; I landed on it." Her voice sounded shaky.

"Are you sure, Eve?" Dad asked.

"I'm sure," Mom said. Dad lifted her to her feet. "We can drive to the Emergency Room," Mom continued. "An ambulance would cost a fortune. Where's Annabel?"

"Watching TV," Dad said. "I don't think she heard the commotion."

"Good," Mom said. "Just tell her I had a little tumble, Stu."

"Mom?" I asked. "How did you trip?"

"It's that stupid carpet," Mom said.

"I keep meaning to fix it," Dad said. "It's my fault."

"Don't be silly," Mom said. "It's my own fault. I was in a hurry, as usual."

It's my fault! I wanted to yell. I grabbed the doll and ran back upstairs. I threw it into my room and heard a sharp squeal as it hit the floor. I slammed the door behind me.

Then I ran back downstairs. Annabel was waiting, wide-eyed, clutching her doll. We all piled into the car to go to the hospital.

Mom called Josie, the waitress, while we were waiting to see the doctor.

"Josie told me not to worry," she said. "It looks like I get a night off." She spoke in a bright voice, but she looked pale and worried.

The doctor finally saw Mom. She had to get X-rays. It turned out that her wrist wasn't broken, only badly sprained.

"Good news," my dad said in relief as the doctor walked away.

"I guess so," Mom said. She turned to Dad. "But Stu, how am I going to cook with my arm in a sling? This could really hurt the restaurant. What are we going to do?"

Dad didn't say anything. Annabel stuck her

thumb in her mouth. She hadn't done that for years.

The Hackett family was in serious trouble. And it was all my fault!

Nobody said much on the way home. Mom held her wrist and stared out the window. Dad drove, his mouth a grim line.

Dad carried Annabel up to her room, and Mom said she was going straight to bed. I hurried upstairs to my room and flung open the door.

The doll was sitting on the desk, its back to me.

I shut the door. "How could you do that?" I whispered furiously. "You could have killed my mom!"

The doll's head rolled all the way around. Now it was sitting backward on its body. The glassy eyes caught the light of the moon. They blinked.

"Cool it, buster," the doll said. "You need a better light on the stairway. She probably tripped on that torn piece of carpet."

"Are you saying you didn't do it?" I demanded. "Do you expect me to believe that?"

"I don't care what you believe," the doll said. "I'm telling you that this house needs a major overhaul. First thing tomorrow you're going to tack that carpet down."

The head swiveled around again toward the window. I took a step toward it. I wanted to tear the doll apart with my bare hands. It would feel so good to throw the pieces into the night.

But what would happen to Mrs. Fink if I did?

I was no fan of El Finko. But now I was responsible for her. I was trapped!

The phone rang out in the hallway. It was past ten o'clock. It was probably Josie, calling to see if Mom was okay.

But Dad bellowed down the hall for me. I stuck my head out.

"It's for you, Jess," he said, frowning. "And it's way too late to be getting calls. Don't stay on long."

I grabbed the phone and took it into the bathroom for privacy. It was Geneva.

"Hey, kiddo," she said, "how's the situation over there?"

I told her about my mom. Geneva sucked in her breath.

"Do you think the doll pushed her?" she whispered.

"I don't know!" I said. "It says she tripped on the carpet. But—"

"I hear you," Geneva said. "How can we know for sure? This situation is seriously out of control."

"We have to get rid of it, Geneva. This calls for desperate measures."

"That's why I'm calling," Geneva said. "I've got good news and bad news. The good news is that I found two spells that can help us. One is called a confinement spell. We can put the doll in a container, and it won't be able to get out."

"That's stellar," I said, relieved.

"We can come over tomorrow and do it," Geneva said. "But the second spell is more complicated." Geneva's voice dropped lower. "We'll be calling up some powerful forces, but I'm willing to give it a shot if you are. If our intent is good, we won't get hurt."

"Okay," I said. "But what do you mean, it's complicated?"

"Well," Geneva said hesitantly, "first of all, we have to do it during the dead hour."

I gulped. "The dead hour?"

"The half hour before midnight and the half hour after midnight," Geneva explained. "The half hour *before* midnight is for casting good spells. That's us. And the half hour *after* is for bad spells."

I bit my lip. "How am I going to get out that late?"

"We'll make up something," Geneva said. "You can have a sleepover with Cody. Then we'll sneak out. My parents sleep like the dead. Whoops, sorry. Anyway, that's not the hard part."

"So what's the hard part?" I asked nervously.

"We need some ingredients for the spell," Geneva said. "A few strands of the real Mrs. Fink's hair, an item of clothing, and a favorite, treasured object of hers."

I blew out a breath. "And how are we supposed to get those things?" I asked. "It's impossible!"

"That brings me to the bad news," Geneva said calmly. "You have to break into Mrs. Fink's house."

12

Breaking In Is Hard to Do

I was up early the next morning. You'd be surprised how quickly a little doll screaming "Get up, sludge-head!" can wake you up.

Dad was making coffee when he saw me walking by with a hammer.

"What's doing?" he asked, yawning. "Work on a Sunday?"

"I want to tack that carpet down," I said.

"Good idea," Dad said, surprised.

Good idea is right. Especially when you have a voodoo doll screaming at you to do it. *And* to replace the bulb in the hall fixture with a bigger wattage. I had forty-five minutes to complete the tasks, eat breakfast, and get back upstairs to work on my history paper.

Mom kissed me when I came down to breakfast. "Thanks for fixing the carpet," she said.

Dad put a plate of his special Mexican scrambled eggs on the table, and everybody helped themselves. Mom passed around a plate of fresh jalapeño corn muffins.

"It's really great how you've been helping out, Jesse," she said to me. She glanced at Dad. "And I hate to say it, but it looks like we're going to have to depend on you even more."

Dad cleared his throat. "Mom and I decided last night that I'm going to work at the restaurant, too. I'm going to quit my night job."

"But how will we pay bills and stuff?" I asked.

"We'll be fine," Dad said in that hearty voice that meant he was trying to talk himself into an idea, too.

"We really have no choice," Mom said.

"We planned that I would quit and do the cooking in the fall," Dad said. "This is just a bit ahead of schedule."

"At least things will be a little less insane around here," Mom said. "With Dad helping, I'll have more free time. We'll have to work at night, but we'll be around during the day."

"But who's going to watch me at night?" Annabel asked.

"Jesse will," Mom said. "He's old enough now." She beamed a smile at me. "And he's been so helpful lately."

"We trust you, Jess," Dad said.

It was a nice thing to hear. Especially since all year I'd messed up.

And, just like that, I realized something. Maybe in some kind of weird way I'd forgotten stuff on purpose. Maybe I wanted to show Mom and Dad that I needed *both* of them around, not just taking turns. I was trying to tell them that their crazy hours couldn't work.

But messing up hadn't helped the situation. It hadn't changed anything. And helping out made me feel better. It made me feel as though we were a team.

As I popped the last piece of muffin into my mouth, I realized something else: If I had to watch Annabel every night, I wouldn't be able to have a sleepover at Cody's house. How could I get away for the final spell?

"Don't sweat it," Geneva said when she and Cody arrived later. "We'll think of something. Let's tackle one problem at a time. Have you decided where you want to put the doll?"

I nodded. "I thought of the perfect place."

This morning, I'd told Annabel I was ready to fix her dollhouse. I'd already moved it into my room. It was a big Victorian number that Mom had bought in a garage sale. There was a floor missing in a bedroom and the bathroom didn't have a door on it. It would take me about ten minutes to fix, but Annabel didn't know that. It could stay in my room for days.

I led Geneva and Cody to my room. I pointed to the dollhouse with my chin. Then I pointed to the closet.

Geneva took out a plastic bag with a bunch of dark roots in it. She sprinkled a tiny bit of the root on every window and door in the dollhouse. Then she took out a tiny carved alligator head that hung on a ribbon.

"This is a ju-ju totem," she whispered, "to ward off evil spirits. Ready?"

"Ready," I said.

Cody sighed. "This is so stupid."

"Just open the closet door," Geneva told him.

Cody opened the door, and he and Geneva quickly scooted behind it. I reached up for the doll. Before it could say anything, I snatched it off the shelf and whisked it into the dollhouse.

The head swiveled. "Nice digs."

I heard Geneva gasp. The closet door slowly swung shut, revealing her and Cody. They shrank against the wall, staring at the doll in horror. Geneva looked as though she were about to faint.

"Hey!" the doll said. "Who are they? You tricked me!"

"Geneva!" I whispered. "Get a grip!"

But instead of getting a grip, Geneva dropped the totem! She was shaking so hard she couldn't hold onto it.

"Geneva!" I yelled.

"I—I—I—" Geneva said. Cody just stood there, his face white.

I snatched up the totem and looked at her wildly. Where was it supposed to go?

"Hey," the doll said. Her eyes flicked from Geneva to Cody. "What's going on?" Then she saw the root sprinkled on the window. "*Aaaaiiii!*" she screamed. "Get it away from me!"

"Geneva!" I yelled desperately.

"O—over the f—front door," Geneva whispered. Quickly, I hung the totem over the dollhouse entrance.

"*Aaaaiiii!*" the doll screamed in that scary, high-pitched voice. "You can't get away with this, Mr. Hackett!" She moved toward the door, then shrank back, as though she'd been burned. She let out a sharp hiss. But she stayed put.

"It worked!" Geneva breathed.

"You weren't sure it would?" I asked incredulously.

"Well, you never know," Geneva said.

"You're saying that *now?*" Cody asked.

I threw a beach towel over the dollhouse so we wouldn't have to look at the doll, who was now baring her teeth at us.

"Okay," I said, "what do we do next?"

"Wait until dark," Geneva said.

Since it was Sunday, the restaurant would close early. So Dad and Mom gave me a break and took Annabel with them to work.

At dusk, Geneva dropped Cody and me off at Mrs. Fink's corner. "Be careful," she said. "Just go in and out. You won't get caught."

"I notice you're taking off," Cody said.

Geneva gave him a withering look. "I have things to do, too. I have to gather some more stuff for the big spell."

"Where are you going?" I asked.

"You don't want to know," Geneva said. She drove off, beads swinging from the rear view mirror.

"I can't believe I'm doing this," Cody said nervously. He gazed up at Mrs. Fink's Victorian house. It looked like a bigger version of Annabel's dollhouse. "I think I should come with you."

"We already decided you'd be the lookout," I said. "It'll be safer that way. Now, we need a signal. If you see anyone coming, make a sound."

"I'll bark like a dog," Cody suggested.

"Perfect," I said.

I looked up at the house. As the shadows lengthened, it looked spookier and spookier. When Cody touched my arm, I jumped.

"Jesse? What if she's...in there?" Cody asked.

"Who?" I said. But I knew who.

"Mrs. Fink," Cody whispered.

"She's not in there," I said uneasily. "Geneva said she wasn't."

"Since when does Geneva make sense?" Cody said. "She's no expert. What if she's wrong? What if Mrs. Fink is lying in there in a coma or something, all stiff and cold..." Cody shivered.

I looked back at the house. What if Geneva *was* wrong? What if Mrs. Fink's body was in the house?

I didn't want to think about it. "Enough talking," I said. "I'm going."

Cody gave me a trembling thumbs-up sign. "Ruff ruff," he said softly.

Keeping near the bushes, I scooted down the driveway to the back of the house. I thought I'd try the basement windows first. With the second window, I hit pay dirt. It swung open with a creak. I crawled inside, then dropped to the floor.

It was just what you'd expect. Even her *basement* was neat. It was clean and swept. Shelves were labeled with canned fruit and vegetables. Boxes were stacked at perfect right angles. Even the toolbox was labeled TOOLBOX.

I tiptoed up the stairs to the main floor. I peeked into the living room and parlor and kitchen. Everything looked normal. There wasn't even any dust. I guessed that dust didn't dare float around Mrs. Fink's house, even when she wasn't there.

It was dark inside. I wished I could turn on a light. And I especially wished Cody hadn't put the thought of a lifeless body into my head.

I went up the carpeted stairway to the second floor. All of the heavy oak doors down the long hall were closed. I hesitated outside the first door. Then I took a deep breath and flung it open.

It was a guest room. Lace curtains filtered the light from a streetlamp right outside.

Ruff ruff! Ruff ruff!

My heart leaped inside my chest. Cody! I raced to the window and peered out. I didn't see Cody, but I *did* see a big black dog in the next-door neighbor's yard barking up a storm.

Whew.

I closed the guest room door and opened the next door. It was a bathroom. I tiptoed across the hall and opened the next. This bedroom was bigger, and I could see it had an adjoining bathroom. A hairbrush and comb and some framed pictures were on the dresser.

This must be Mrs. Fink's room.

Ruff ruff!

That dog again. But this time I heard the *yip yip* of another dog. I hurried to the back window and peeked out. There was a small collie in the backyard of the next house over. It was barking in answer to the big black dog.

Great. How would I hear Cody in all this noise? I'd better hustle.

I looked around again and gasped. It was horrible. It was the weirdest thing I'd ever seen!

Whoever would have imagined that Mrs. Fink would collect...*teddy bears!*

I circled around the room, checking out shelves and tabletops. Teddy bears with clothes. Teddy bears with ribbons. Old teddy bears. New teddy bears.

They lined the shelves and stared out at me with unblinking glassy eyes. And you can guess how I felt about *that.*

Another dog had joined the neighborhood chorus as I picked up a silver hairbrush. It would probably contain enough gray hairs for Geneva to work with. I shoved it in my jacket pocket. Then I opened the closet door. Any item of clothing would do, Geneva had said. Even something small, like a handkerchief.

That's when I heard them—sirens.

The police!

13

When the Moon Becomes Round

I ran back to the window. I peeked out just in time to see a police car screech into Mrs. Fink's driveway.

Someone must have seen me. Or maybe Mrs. Fink had one of those silent alarm systems. It didn't matter. My goose was cooked.

I grabbed the sash from a plaid robe and stuffed it in the pocket of my jacket. I started out of the room, but then stopped with a jerk.

The treasured object! I couldn't leave without it. But what should I take?

My eyes lighted on the teddy bear in the middle of the bed. It looked older and more worn than the others. I snatched it up and took off.

I hit the bottom of the stairs as heavy boots hit the porch. The doorknob rattled.

I careered down the hall and threw myself

down the basement stairs. I hoisted myself up to the window and wiggled through.

A flashlight beam snaked down the driveway. I backed up. My foot hit something squishy.

"Ow," Cody breathed.

"Where *were* you?" I whispered furiously. "Why didn't you give the signal?"

"I *did!*" Cody whispered back. "But every single dog in the neighborhood was barking, too. How could you hear me through the pooch chorus?"

Footsteps were coming down the driveway. "I'd say it's time to split," Cody said.

We streaked across the lawn and squirmed through a hole in the hedge. Then we cut across somebody's back lawn. The sound of barking dogs was still in our ears as we finally hit the street and slowed to a walk. We'd made it!

"Great haul," Geneva said as I threw the items on Cody's bed. She tossed down some plastic bags filled with weird-looking stuff. "I was lucky, too."

"So when can we do it?" I said. "Soon?"

Geneva sat cross-legged on the floor. She tossed her long braid behind her shoulder. "We can't do it until Wednesday night."

"*Wednesday?*" Cody said. "That's three whole days away!"

I groaned. "It's a *lifetime* away."

"Sorry, guys," Geneva said, "but the spell is clear. It has to be performed during a full moon." She reached into her purse and pulled out a thick, dusty book. She flipped it open and scanned a passage. "'When the moon becomes round,'" she read. "You see?"

"I see," I said, looking over her shoulder.

"It's not too bad," Geneva said cheerfully. "The doll is safely locked up. And it's only three days away. It could have been weeks."

"I guess you're right," Cody said.

"Easy for you guys to say," I said. "The doll isn't your roommate. You don't have to listen to what it says..."

Geneva looked at me. "What does it say, Jesse?" she asked softly.

I shrugged. "Stuff. Like everything that happened is my fault. That it picked me because I have bad thoughts."

Geneva leaned close. "Don't listen to it, Jesse. That would be very dangerous. Look, there's nobody on this whole planet who doesn't have bad thoughts sometimes. And there's something else. The doll could only take over a person whose life energy was low. Someone who *wanted* to give up on life. So you could say it's Mrs. Fink's fault, too."

"But it *wasn't* her fault!" I protested. "The doll *used* her."

"Exactly my point," Geneva said. "It's using you, too. So don't feel guilty. It will just get in the way. You have a very important role to play during the final spell."

"What do you mean?" I asked uneasily. "I thought you were going to do it."

"I'll do most of it," Geneva said. "But you're the keeper of the doll. You have to get rid of it. The book says you have to show a pure intent."

"What does *that* mean?" I asked.

"I'm not sure," Geneva said, "but I guess we'll find out. In three days, we meet at the edge of the woods at the town beach. Jesse, you bring the doll. I'll bring the other stuff."

The three of us nodded solemnly. Geneva sighed. "Now we just have one more thing to worry about."

"What now?" Cody asked.

"We've got to see the moon," Geneva said. "So just pray it doesn't rain."

I moved the dollhouse into the closet. That way, I only had to listen to the doll scream at me when I got my robe or something. I slept better that night than I had in days.

When I opened the closet door the next morning, the doll was awake, waiting for me.

"Did you finish your paper?" she asked.

"Good morning to you, too," I said, grabbing my sweatshirt.

"Don't you think I should look it over for you?"

"Why?" I asked.

"Look at it this way, Hackett," the doll said. "I took over your teacher. You might say I know what she knows. Don't *you* want to know what she'd say?"

The doll had a point. I slipped the paper inside the dollhouse and left to wash up.

I came back in, whistling. "So?" I called. "Was it a stellar piece of work, or what?"

"Mmmmffff," the doll said.

I whipped my head around. The doll was chewing. As I watched, the last page of my history paper disappeared inside its mouth. The doll had eaten my homework!

14

The Dark Side

A narrow red tongue snaked out as the doll licked her lips. "What did you expect? You locked me up. You have to learn that I'm still the boss!"

Not for long, I thought. I slammed the closet door shut, snatched up my knapsack, and took off for school.

Before class, I went up to Ms. Macro and told her my paper wasn't done. I explained about my mom's trip to the emergency room and my dad quitting his job.

"That's fine, Jesse," Ms. Macro said. "Things are so topsy-turvy with Mrs. Fink gone anyway. You can have until Wednesday."

"Wow, Ms. Macro, that's really nice," I said. "Mrs. Fink never cut me any slack."

"Did you ever tell her *why* you didn't do your homework?" Ms. Macro asked. "Like you just did with me?"

97

"She wouldn't understand," I said. "You're easy to talk to." Ms. Macro wore bright red lipstick and tied her fuzzy blond hair into a ponytail. She joked with the kids and even played basketball. She was cool.

Ms. Macro smiled at me. "Mrs. Fink has been teaching a long time," she said. "Maybe she's a little out of touch with today's students, but maybe they don't give her a break, either."

"I don't know," I said. "Maybe."

Ms. Macro closed her binder. "And I'll tell you something else. The students in Mrs. Fink's classes pull the best grades in school."

"That's because they're scared not to," I said.

Ms. Macro shrugged. "Whatever works."

The bell rang, and everyone filed into class. I tried to pay attention, but I couldn't stop thinking about Mrs. Fink. Geneva had said that her life energy must have been low. That's why she was a pushover for the doll. Part of her *wanted* to let go of life.

But part of Mrs. Fink must be still around, I thought suddenly. It was Mrs. Fink who was making me do my work, organizing my chores. Hadn't the doll said that it knew what Mrs. Fink knew? *Mrs. Fink was in there, somewhere.*

So if she could reach *me,* why couldn't I reach her?

Suddenly, I raised my hand, right in the middle of Debbi Oleander's report.

"Yes, Jesse?" Ms. Macro said.

"I'm sorry to interrupt," I said, "but I just had an idea. I think the class should get together and do something to welcome Mrs. Fink back. When she comes back."

Burt Mackinac turned around and gave me an incredulous look. I guess it *was* pretty weird for me to be welcoming Mrs. Fink back.

But Ms. Macro seemed pleased. "That's a very nice idea, Jesse," she said. "We'll talk about it after Debbi's report."

Debbi droned on, but I wasn't listening at all. I didn't know if I *could* reach Mrs. Fink. But I would try. I would let her know that people missed her. Maybe I could convince her that it was worth the fight to get back.

Over the next couple of days, the doll ruled my life. It lectured and ordered and jeered. It laughed at me and yelled at me. Every night, I heard the voice in my dreams.

But the funny thing was, even though I was haunted, my life was working out. The house ran smoothly. Annabel was no trouble. Since Dad and Mom were working side by side, they were in better moods. I did my history paper over, and it was better. I'd been too careless the first time.

Meanwhile, I was working hard on the surprise for Mrs. Fink. I got all the kids in school to sign a big "Welcome Home" banner. Cristina Spinola wrote "Get well soon" in Portuguese. I even dropped by the library to ask the librarian if the little kids Mrs. Fink read to on Saturdays would contribute drawings.

Geneva talked to the kids in high school who'd survived Mrs. Fink's class years ago. It was funny, but lots of them wanted to help. A couple of kids said Mrs. Fink was the reason they had good study habits now. They all dropped by the middle school to sign the banner.

On Wednesday, I finally read my paper to the class. Ms. Macro said she was completely knocked out. "Fascinating *and* informative," she told me.

My first A! It was weird what could happen when you concentrated.

Cody caught up with me after school. "Stellar paper," he said. "You aced it."

"Thanks," I said. "Are you ready for tonight?"

Cody nodded. "All set."

We had worked everything out beforehand.

Dad and Mom were keeping the restaurant open later these days to get more customers. They didn't get home until way after midnight. If Cody came over to stay with Annabel, I could go with Geneva to the town beach.

Cody wasn't crazy about missing out, but he'd agreed it was the only way. Maybe he was a little relieved, too.

Cody looked up at the sky. "I hope the weather holds, though. It looks awfully cloudy."

"But we can't wait!" I cried.

"We might have to," Cody replied. "The moon will be full tomorrow night, too."

I looked so crushed that Cody punched me in the arm. "Don't worry about it," he said. "It'll probably clear up."

Just as he said that, a big drop of rain fell on my nose.

After my parents left for work, I went up to my room. I unfurled the banner carefully. Then I opened the closet door.

The doll blinked. "What's that?"

"It's for Mrs. Fink," I said casually. "All her students signed it."

"Roll it up!" the doll shrieked. "Now!"

"I don't want to tear it," I said.

"Do it!" the doll screamed.

But instead, I pushed it closer. "I never knew so many kids cared about Mrs. Fink," I said.

The doll scuttled forward and pressed against the window of the dollhouse. "I am not to be trifled with," she croaked. "I am to be *feared*. I am more powerful than you could imagine in any dark dream."

Her eyes burned into mine. It was like the first time I'd seen the doll in the shop. My feet seemed glued to the floor.

The thought seared my brain. *We're in this together. Forever.*

"That's right," the doll said. "You think you have me trapped. But mark me, Mr. Hackett. You are in my power, as is she. I know how strong your bad side is. I know your every evil wish."

The eyes seemed to peer into my very soul. They saw every mean thought, every selfish wish, I'd ever had. They saw how tired I was of watching Annabel. How jealous I was of Cody's straight A's. How angry I was that my parents worked all the time. It understood everything, and it *approved*.

Don't listen to it, Geneva had said.

But how could I not? It *knew* me.

"Why do you think your mother fell down

the stairs?" the doll said softly. "Didn't you want her to? Didn't you want her to fail at her business? Whose fault do *you* think it was?"

"No!" I shouted. It took all of my willpower, but I shut the closet door.

15

Kidnapped

I had to get rid of it. If I didn't, it would destroy me.

That night, the hours crawled by. It seemed to take forever to cook dinner, clean up, and get Annabel to bed. But finally she was asleep, and I was alone. Waiting.

I turned on the TV and tried to watch it. I kept listening for the sound of rain. It had stopped drizzling a while ago, but the sky was still cloudy.

Cody was supposed to show up at about eleven fifteen. His parents always fell asleep in the middle of the news. At ten to eleven, I heard a noise. I sprang up with relief. Cody was early.

But when I walked into the front hall, Annabel was coming down the stairs.

"What are you doing out of bed?" I demanded.

"I had a bad dream," Annabel said.

"Get right back upstairs," I ordered. "Now."

Annabel started to cry. "But I'm scared! Will you play Go Fish with me?"

"Will I *what?*" I said. "No way!"

Then Annabel really started to cry. If she got wound up, she could go on for hours.

"Okay, okay," I said. "One hand. Then back in bed. Promise?"

Annabel sniffed. "Promise."

We went back in the den. I got out the cards and dealt them. But I was freaked, thinking that Cody would show up any minute. I couldn't concentrate.

"Hey," Annabel said, "you said you didn't have any threes. You're cheating."

"I'm not cheating," I said. "I just didn't see them. Here." I pushed the cards toward her.

"And you said you'd fix my dollhouse, and you haven't," Annabel said.

"I'm working on it," I snapped.

"I win!" Annabel crowed.

"Okay," I said, "back to bed."

Annabel's lower lip stuck out. "One more . hand."

"No way," I said. "We had a deal."

"But you weren't paying attention," Annabel cried. "It's not fair!"

"I don't care!" I said. "Get upstairs. Now."

"You can't tell me what to do," Annabel said.

"You're not my daddy. I want my daddy," she said, her lower lip quivering.

"Well, he's not here, so get moving," I said.

Was that rain tapping against the windowpane? Or was Cody arriving? I couldn't tell. I wished Annabel would stop whimpering.

"Will you get lost!" I snapped at Annabel.

Tears formed in Annabel's big brown eyes. "I'm going," she said haughtily. "I'd rather talk to my dolls than talk to you!"

"If you're not asleep in five minutes, you're in big trouble," I warned.

"I don't care!" Annabel shouted over her shoulder as she stomped up the stairs.

As soon as Annabel disappeared into her room, I ran out the front door. I looked up at the sky. The clouds covered the moon. It hadn't been rain that I'd heard, or Cody. It had been the wind. The trees whispered spookily as the breeze skittered through the leaves.

I closed the front door and paced back and forth. Things were still okay, I told myself. Annabel was in bed. I'd check on her in a minute. It was so late she was probably already asleep. I went in the kitchen to check the clock. I saw that I'd forgotten to turn on the dishwasher. I scraped our dessert plates and put them in, then turned on the machine. I wiped the counter. Eleven-ten. Where was Cody?

I crept up the stairs, praying Annabel was already asleep. I eased open her door.

Her bed was empty.

"Annabel?" I said. "Stop playing games."

No answer.

"Look, I'm sorry I yelled," I said. "Come on out. I'll give you another cookie," I wheedled.

No answer. I looked under the bed and in the closet. Then I checked the bathroom. No Annabel.

I stopped in the middle of the hall as a chill gripped my heart. What had Annabel said before she went upstairs?

I'd rather talk to my dolls...

I crossed to my room and threw open the door. The alligator totem was on the floor along with the dried roots. The dollhouse was empty.

The doll was gone. And so was Annabel!

16

Hour of the Dead

"Don't panic," I told myself out loud.

Annabel could still be in the house. Or she could have taken the doll over to her friend Julie Baxter's.

I pounded back down the stairs and searched the house. Then I called the Baxters next door. I knew Mrs. Baxter was a night owl.

"No, Annabel isn't here," Mrs. Baxter said. Her voice was concerned. "Is everything okay, Jesse?"

"Of course," I said quickly. "She, um, had a bad dream, and I went to get her some warm milk. Now she's hiding. She's probably under the bed—heh, heh—well, what do you know, here she is. You're a bad girl, Annabel. Yes, I'll put you to bed. Thanks, Mrs. Baxter. Sorry to bother you."

"No bother, dear," Mrs. Baxter said.

I tore outside. A slight drizzle was falling. I slipped on the wet grass as I dashed to the garage and looked inside. I ran down the street in one direction, then the other. I didn't see a little girl in a fluffy pink robe. And I didn't see a scary voodoo doll walking beside her.

I circled back toward my house just as Cody hurried across the lawn to my front door. He was dressed in his yellow slicker, and he shook off raindrops as I came up.

"Sorry I'm late," he said. "My parents took forever to go to sleep. I just came over to tell you that Geneva called the whole thing off. The weather is too awful."

"She can't call it off!" I panted.

"Tomorrow's supposed to be clear," Cody said. "It's just one more day, Jesse."

"Cody, Annabel is missing!" I yelled. "And she's with the doll!"

Cody's mouth dropped open. "How did that happen?"

"I'll explain later," I said. "There's no time now. We have to do the spell anyway. The doll is probably furious at being locked up in the dollhouse. What if she takes it out on Annabel?"

"Oh, my gosh," Cody said.

"Let's go," I said. "We have to get Geneva."

Cody looked at me, horrified. "But we can't. Geneva called me from a concert. She said she won't be home for another hour."

"But we'll miss the dead hour!" I exclaimed. I thought fast. "We have no choice. We have to do the spell ourselves."

Cody's face went pale. Then slowly he nodded.

Cody and I hurried back to his house. I waited outside while he eased open the back door and sneaked in. In a few minutes, he reappeared with Geneva's bag.

"I found everything," he whispered. "All the roots and stuff. And the book of spells. Do you think the spell will work if you don't have the doll?"

"I don't know," I said. "But I have to try."

We raced down the wet streets toward the bay. When we got to the town beach, there were only fifteen minutes left until midnight.

"We don't have much time," I said worriedly. "After midnight, the spell won't work."

The beach was dark and deserted. It had stopped raining, and the sky was a gleaming gray, like a pearl. Every so often the clouds would part, and I'd glimpse the moon. Maybe it was clearing up!

Geneva had included a small flashlight with the other items. Cody trained it on the book while he read through the instructions. "The first thing we have to do is build a fire," he said.

"I hope we can," I said. "Everything is so wet."

We hurried into the woods and gathered up the driest wood we could find. Then we dug a shallow pit and dumped the wood in. I checked my watch while Cody fished in Geneva's bag for matches. Five minutes to go.

Geneva had even thrown in some old newspaper to get the fire going. Cody handed me the book and flashlight. "Here," he said. "You read the steps while I get this lit."

I pored over the book while Cody lit match after match. It was lucky he hadn't flunked out of Boy Scouts like I had. Soon, he had coaxed a small fire.

"Okay," I muttered. "Here we go."

I took a round brass bowl from Geneva's bag and crumbled some roots in it. Then I added the gray hairs that I combed out of Mrs. Fink's hairbrush. I plucked some threads from the sash of the robe and added them. Then I looked through Geneva's plastic bags for the next ingredient.

"Cody, get this," I said softly as I shook out some dirt into the bowl. "Dirt taken from a grave. That's where Geneva went that night."

Cody shivered. "You don't have to keep me posted on *everything,* Hackett."

I sounded out some weird incantation from the book. I didn't recognize any of the words. Suddenly, the fire died down. Then it flared up again, hotter than before.

"Did you see that?" Cody whispered.

"Maybe it's working," I said.

"Hurry," Cody said. "It's one minute to midnight."

"I have to hold the bowl up until it catches a ray of the round moon," I said, reading. "The moon has to shine on it. And then I'm supposed to throw the treasured object into the fire."

"Jesse," Cody said. His voice was shaking. "Look."

I looked into the fire. A face had appeared in the flames. It was the doll!

"Don't do it, Jesse," it said. It wasn't the doll's usual croak. This voice was soft and lilting.

"Don't go on," the doll said coaxingly. "You'll destroy me if you do. You'll destroy the best part of yourself."

"It's a trick," Cody said.

I hesitated. My hand gripped the bowl. "What should I do?" I hissed to Cody.

"I don't know," Cody said, scared.

"Think, Jesse," the doll said. "Think how I helped you."

"You tripped my mom," I said. "You took Annabel!"

"Your mother tripped on the carpet," the doll said in the same lulling voice. "And Annabel left on her own. I have her safe, Jesse."

"Where?" I demanded.

The doll didn't answer me. "Remember what I've done for you. Your household is organized. Your parents are proud of you. You did well in school. Think, Jesse. Think about how much better your life is with me beside you."

"Jesse, don't listen," Cody said. "Remember what Geneva said. You have to be clear!"

But I *wasn't* clear. I was confused. Was the doll so bad? Everything it said was true.

"I am not evil," the doll said. "No more than you. We can work together."

"Jesse!" Cody yelled again. "It's Annabel!"

I looked across the fire, down the beach. Annabel was walking down the pier toward the water.

"Put down the bowl, Jesse," the doll said. "You see my power? Annabel can stay on the dock, or she can fall in the water. Do not betray me. We are together. You called me, and I came to you. And now you need me."

I heard a voice behind me, and I turned. It was Geneva. She was racing down the beach, her orange skirt flying. "Do it, Jesse!" she screamed. "Do it now!"

But it was like she was in a dream. Her words seemed to float toward me. They took a long time. I turned back to the flames.

I stared at the doll. Maybe I *had* called it. Maybe I *did* need it.

I lowered the bowl.

"You are tired of your sister anyway," the doll said soothingly, hypnotically. "She's always in the way. Isn't she, Jesse?"

I looked across the fire. The smoke stung my eyes, but I could make out Annabel on the end of the pier. And heading toward her was the doll, walking stiffly, her jointed arms outstretched.

"Jesse!" Geneva screamed.

I held the bowl up to the sky.

Blue flames shot up from the fire. The clouds parted. A shaft of moonlight hit the bowl, and it began to glow.

Suddenly, the doll reappeared in the fire.

"*Noooooo!*" it screamed. "*Stop!*"

I held the teddy bear close to the flames.

"*No!*" the doll screamed.

I threw the bear into the fire.

The flames shot forward, blinding me for an instant. Then I saw the doll's face. It was starting to melt. Its hideous mouth opened wide in a soundless scream.

"Save me, Jesse," the doll said.

I took a running step toward the fire.

"Jesse, don't!" Geneva yelled behind me.

But I was already leaping toward the flames.

17

Hocus Pocus

I heard Cody gasp as I cleared the licking flames. I barely touched down on the other side of the fire before I was off, flying toward the pier.

Annabel stood at the very edge, facing the sea. Her dark curls bobbed in the breeze. But now, a tall form stood next to her, with a hand on Annabel's shoulder. It was Mrs. Fink!

I pounded down the wooden slats of the pier. "Annabel!" I called.

"Jesse!" Annabel ran toward me. I bent down, and she ran into my arms. "I wasn't scared," she said.

"Scared of what?" I asked.

"Of being lost," Annabel said. "Well, maybe I was in the beginning. But then I found this lady, and she was lost, too!"

I looked up. Mrs. Fink stood in front of me. She looked dazed. 'She was weaving a little, clutching a slightly singed teddy bear. It was the one I'd just thrown into the fire!

Annabel looked up at me. "It's not really my fault," she said. "You *told* me to get lost."

"It's okay," I said. "Are you all right, Mrs. Fink?"

"I—I think so, Jesse," she said. "What are you doing here? What am *I* doing here?"

"I was looking for Annabel," I said as Geneva and Cody ran up. "Where have you been?"

Mrs. Fink passed a hand over her forehead. "I don't really know."

"Is everyone okay?" Geneva asked. She crouched down until she was eye-level with Annabel. "And what happened to you?"

"I got mad at Jesse," Annabel said. "While he was starting the dishwasher, I stole his doll and sneaked out the door. But it was really dark, and I got kind of scared. I don't know what happened next. I guess I got lost. Because all of a sudden I was here!"

"And then?" Geneva asked gently.

Annabel frowned. "I thought I heard somebody telling me to walk toward the water. So I went all the way to the end of the pier. But then I heard this noise behind me, and it was this old lady."

"Don't call her an old lady, Annabel," I said.

"It's all right," Mrs. Fink said. "She saved my life. I was in some kind of trance."

Geneva stood up. "I think we'd better get Annabel home," she said. "I had a funny feeling at the concert that something was wrong. I knew I was psychic!"

"Why don't you come home with us, Mrs. Fink," I said. "If you don't mind my saying so, you don't look so hot."

"If you don't mind my saying so, I don't *feel* so hot," Mrs. Fink said.

We all walked toward Geneva's truck. Mrs. Fink and Annabel got in the cab, and Cody and I sat in the back. I watched the dark water recede as we headed across the parking lot. I could just make out the dying smoke of the fire.

It was all over.

When we got home, Mom and Dad were a wreck. They'd found an empty house, and they panicked. They'd already called the Glimchers and the Baxters and were just about to call the police.

I tried to explain what had happened while Annabel interrupted me every five minutes. Geneva and Cody took off to reassure their parents that they were okay.

"I don't know who to be more angry at, you

or Annabel," Mom said helplessly. "I guess I'll have to decide tomorrow," she said, suddenly drawing us to her in a hug.

"Let's all sit down in the kitchen," Dad suggested. "I bet Mrs. Fink could use a cup of tea."

"That sounds heavenly," Mrs. Fink said.

Everyone sat around the kitchen table while Mom put the kettle on and got out the teapot.

"How long have I been away?" Mrs. Fink asked, pressing her hand to her forehead. "That must have been some knock on the head. I don't remember a thing."

"You've been gone almost a week," I said. "We all thought you'd gone to Wyoming to stay with your nephew."

"I guess nobody missed me, then," Mrs. Fink said. Her gray eyes suddenly looked misty.

"Hold on a minute," I said. I charged up the stairs and got the six-foot-long banner. I brought it back downstairs and unfurled it on the floor.

Mrs. Fink walked all the way around it. She reached down to touch a name here and there. And then she saw Cristina's message in Portuguese.

"That's one of the last things I remember," she said. "I felt bad about correcting Cristina's pronunciation so sternly. I met her mother in the hospital—she's a nurse. They speak Portuguese at home. Cristina studies hard, but she's still struggling with English."

"It's okay, Mrs. Fink," I said. "Cristina might be scared of you. But at least her English is better."

"That's nice of you to say, Jesse," Mrs. Fink said. She sighed.

"Annabel, I think it's bedtime," Dad said.

"Can I stay up with everybody?" Annabel pleaded. "Please? I'm not one bit sleepy."

Dad hesitated. "Okay. Just this once. I guess you and Jesse can go to school a little later tomorrow. Is that okay, Mrs. Fink?"

"I have a feeling I'll be a little late myself," Mrs. Fink said.

"I'll bring them to school after I go to the docks for the fish," Dad said.

"No, you have to go to the bank to see about the loan," Mom said, frowning. "Maybe I'll bake the pies here in the morning instead of at the cafe. Then I can drive the kids."

"Or I can go after the bank," Dad offered. "I'll have to skip the grocery shopping, though. Jesse, can you stop by the store after school? You can pick up stuff for dinner."

"Sure," I said.

"My, my," Mrs. Fink said. "What a busy family. It's a wonder it all runs so smoothly."

Mom laughed as she poured tea into Mrs. Fink's cup. "It doesn't," she said. "But thanks to everybody pitching in, we manage to limp along."

"No wonder Jesse finds it hard to concentrate," Mrs. Fink said. She stirred her tea thoughtfully. "The world has changed so much since I started teaching. I guess I got out of step."

"Maybe the kids didn't help any, Mrs. Fink," I said. "Like me, for instance."

Mrs. Fink's gray eyes warmed. "Maybe we both need to bend a little. Right, Mr. Hackett?"

"Right," I said.

"I'm hungry," Annabel announced suddenly.

Mom laughed. "Me, too. How about some ham-and-cheese omelettes?"

"I could use a bite of something," Mrs. Fink said.

Mom got up to make omelettes. Mrs. Fink smiled at Annabel. "I'd like to thank you for taking care of me tonight, Annabel." She handed Annabel her teddy bear. "This is my very favorite antique stuffed animal. I want you to have it."

"Really?" Annabel breathed. "It's so cute!"

I looked at the bear. It was sort of cuddly, I guess, but I'd never be a sucker for a stuffed animal again. There was something about those glass eyes that would probably spook me for the rest of my life.

Annabel hugged the bear closer. One of the eyes slowly closed in a wink.

Whoa. Wait a second. Had Annabel made the hinged eye close, or had it closed all by itself?

Of course Annabel did it, I told myself.

"Jesse? Can you give me a hand?" Mom pointed toward the cutting board with her chin. "Will you slice some apples for me?" she asked.

"Sure," I said. I put an apple on the board and reached for the paring knife. I carefully sliced off a piece.

"Something about the face on that bear is very unusual," Mom said. "Where did you get it, Mrs. Fink?"

"At this odd little shop in St. Jude," Mrs. Fink said.

The knife slipped, and I cut my finger.

"Ow!" I said. I dashed toward the sink.

"Jesse, are you all right?" Mom asked, hurrying toward me. She examined my finger as she held it under the cold water. "It doesn't look bad," she said, relieved.

"It's fine," I said numbly.

I wrapped a napkin around the cut. When I turned around, I noticed the bear. Annabel had put it on the empty chair next to her. There was a bandage on its right paw. Had it been there before?

The bear continued to stare at me with the same glassy gaze. Only this time, the light in the kitchen caught the eyes in a way that made them look almost real. Then the bear's eye slowly closed in a wink.

The hair rose on the back on my neck. Because this time, Annabel wasn't touching the bear at all.

It was sitting all by itself....

**Don't miss the next book in the
Shadow Zone series:
SKELETON IN MY CLOSET**

I took a deep breath and eased through the hole in my closet wall. On the other side was a small, dusty room.

I heard the shuffling noise again.

Then something caught my eye. Something white. In a moment I realized what it was. The bones of a foot!

Slowly, my gaze traveled up a shinbone to a knee...A thigh...Ribs...And then the hideous grin of a dark-eyed skull.

It was a skeleton!